31

STILL EXPLOSION

A LAURA MALLOY MYSTERY

MARY LOGUE

To Erin—
I've enjoyed reading
your work so much—
hope you like this.
keep in touch.
yours,
Mary

SEAL PRESS

Design by Clare Conrad
Cover Art by Debbie Hanley

Library of Congress Cataloging-in-Publication Data

Logue, Mary.
  Still Explosion / Mary Logue.
    p.   cm.
  ISBN 1-878067-29-X
  I. Title.
PS3562.0456S75   1993   92-43990
813'.54—dc20   CIP

Printed in the United States of America
First printing, May 1993
10 9 8 7 6 5 4 3 2 1

Foreign Distribution:
In Canada: Raincoast Book Distribution, Vancouver, B.C.
In Great Britain and Europe: Airlift Book Company, London.

Acknowledgements

I would like to thank the following people for helping me on the research of this book: David Indrehus, Diane Hellekson, Katherine Lanpher and Raymond DiPrima.

*This book is dedicated with love to my comrades
in crime-writing—The Suspenders:*

R.D. Zimmerman

Kate Green

Stephen Cohen

1

THERE IS a stillness that surrounds a blast, whether it's an actual explosion or a dropped sentence that kills. You know what I mean. Like a breath around it that sets that moment apart from the rest of your life. It's framed in silence, an absence of the senses, and everything stops. I've had it happen both ways to me and they're not moments I'll ever forget.

It started on a day in early April, 9:30 a.m. April was certainly a cruel month in Minnesota, with snow hiding in shadows on the lawns like forgotten fears. I was ready to do an interview, standing on the street, the sky liquid with the softest morning light. The Lakewood Family Planning Clinic in St. Paul had already been open over an hour and this was when the director had agreed to talk to me. But I had to cross the street and brave the cluster of protesters who were handing out pamphlets and harassing the women who entered the clinic. This was one of the reasons I had chosen this clinic—out of all the clinics in Minnesota they were getting the most flak from the anti-abortion groups.

I put my head down and walked straight ahead toward the door of the clinic. When I was within yards of it, someone put a hand on my arm. I stopped and looked at a woman who I guessed was my age, but she wore her skin like it was a shapeless dress.

"Get your hand off me," I said and instead of moving away from her, pushed into her. It worked. She stepped back and released my arm.

"Baby killer," she hissed at me.

After I walked past her, I found myself surpressing the urge to turn and stick my tongue out at her. But I knew this was no kid's game. The air around the clinic was charged.

A gray-uniformed guard was sitting at a desk in front of the interior door to the clinic and had me sign in. This semblance of a security system made sense. There had been trouble. That's why I was down there. To find out what was going on and write a feature story on it. The Supreme Court with its latest ruling had virtually handed the abortion issue back to the states and I was going to do a piece on what people in Minnesota thought of this decision and how it would affect them.

As I walked through the waiting room and approached the receptionist, I was going over questions in my mind. The dark-haired girl looked up at me and I told her I was Laura Malloy and flashed my *Twin Cities Times* press card. She nodded and smiled. I remember her smile more than I remember her. After all, it was a Monday morning and I was surprised that someone could smile so fully at the beginning of the week. The smile showed off a few crooked teeth, but was all the more charming for the flaws. I'm sure I was smiling back at her as I turned and looked around the room.

There were about eight woman waiting, some with men. They were all ages and appeared to be from all income levels. One in particular I noticed. She looked like a lawyer with her trim blue suit and a briefcase at her feet. Short dark brown hair, a big pair of glasses on her nose. She was actually working on something. I thought of coming back out after my interview with the director and trying to talk to some of them. I'd like to find out what had brought them to this point in their lives and how they would feel if this right were taken away from them. But I moved through the waiting room and pushed open the swinging door.

There was a thud as I hit the swinging door with my shoulder. A muffled thud, not much of a sound. Then I moved past the door and into the hallway. I have told the rest of this a million times and I can only remember what my mind had time to capture, the little camera lenses of my eyes flashing on a few things.

The receptionist had said the director's office was down at the end of the hall. There were three doors along the right side of the hallway and a ratty beige carpet on the floor. I stopped for a moment when I was just through the door to go over my first angle. I never start an interview out with a question, instead I comment on something like the weather, something we can agree on.

But I had also stopped because there was one other person in the hallway, a young man, and he surprised me. It was odd the way he was standing, hesitant. He was bent over and was holding what looked like a rolled-up newspaper in his hands. He glanced up at me and I saw his dark eyes and the faint memory of a smile. That was it.

Then the world erupted in front of me. The air blew apart and produced a roar that peaked into unhearable dimensions, as if every molecule of oxygen were shrieking as it ripped apart. The air was grabbed from my mouth and I was spun around, knocked over, then pushed back through the doors. My notebook flew from my hands and I hit my head on the linoleum floor of the waiting room. The doors sucked back in and I rolled away from the force.

Right afterward it was so quiet all I could hear was the shush, shush of my heart pushing blood through my neck.

I was staring at a perforated ceiling and one of the doors was hanging from its hinges. I could hear thin cries, like mice squealing, but I knew it was the women behind me. I crawled to my knees and looked down the hallway. A deep, sulfurous smell was oozing down the hall, low to the floor. The air was filled with fine white powder, like the snow that comes when it's below zero. But I could see that someone had sprayed graffiti on the side walls of the hallway, long red streaks, and I wondered if the marks meant anything.

I was up on my feet and moving before I had time to think. It was as if I were pulled in by the aftershock. After I went through the one door left hanging, I reached out and touched the wall to steady myself. That was when I saw the stress cracks like skinny rivers running across the plaster surface. I took my hand away and kept going. I had this thought in my mind that I wanted to read the graffiti, thinking it would tell me something. And then I got there. The red smears I ignored, it was the body I stared at.

There was another explosion then, but it was soundless and inside of me. As a cop reporter I had seen too many dead bodies, but I had never seen anything like this one before. At my feet was the young man. His face was twisted back and he appeared to be staring at the ceiling. His eyes were open and now I could see they were dark brown. They made him seem alive and I felt hope when I knew there was none. His hands were missing, the arms of his coat were shredded like the ends of a firecracker. His legs were pushed up against the wall and where his stomach and chest should have been was a pool of blood. Like a doll that had been caught in a game of tug of war, his two ends were no longer connected. Because the middle of his body was gone.

And then I started to hear tinny footsteps. Two women were picking their way carefully down the hall. I wanted them to go away. I reached down and touched the man's cheek. It was already covered with a thin coat of dust. Rice-powder makeup. He looked so fragile. He had been alive when I stepped into the hallway. He had been moving. Then he had blown up. The sound of his death echoed and echoed in my ears. It was all I could hear.

An older woman, all dressed in white, squatted down and felt for a pulse on the side of the man's neck. Then she turned and put an arm around me. "He's dead," she whispered. Her words sounded like they were coming down a tunnel.

"I know," I said. "I think we better keep everyone out of here. The police...." I trailed off. My own voice sounded distant, like someone else was talking right behind me.

She motioned to the other woman to go back and kept an arm around me, walking me down the hall. My coat had been half pulled off of me. I knew I must look a mess. She seemed to be talking to me, but it was just a murmur, a soothing undercurrent that didn't make any sense. I couldn't stop seeing the body, it blinked in front of my eyes, red from blood, white from the flash. The explosion. It had been a bomb. I guess I knew that as soon as it had happened. Blink, red, blink, bomb. Life, death. Here one second, blown up the next. I concentrated on walking and breathing.

In the reception area women were grouped together. Some were crying, I could see their shoulders shaking, see them rubbing their eyes. The dark-haired lawyer was consoling a younger woman who was doubled over in her chair. I thought about crying, but I didn't seem to have it in me. The receptionist was on the phone. The woman in white, she was a nurse I assumed, sat me down on the end of a couch. She squatted in front of me and looked me in the eyes. She reminded me of a Scandinavian housekeeper:

big broad face, large hands, eyes that were as blue as a fjord. I trusted her.

"Are you all right?" she asked.

Again she sounded as if she were miles away. I shook my head, my ears felt clogged up, like they had water in them.

"You're not all right?" she asked.

"I'm not hearing very well, but I don't think I got hurt." I looked down at myself. I was covered with dust, my back hurt from landing on the ground, but I just felt numb, blasted out. "Who was he?"

"He was here with his girlfriend."

The woman took my head in her hands and started to check me over.

"Does she know?" I asked.

"No, she's not out yet. She's getting an abortion."

2

THE AMBULANCE attendants came in first. The older
woman, after being sure I was all right, went and
talked to them. I could see them looking down the hallway
and shaking their heads. I knew she was saying, don't even
bother. And they knew enough to let the body be. The
cops would appreciate it.

Then the bomb squad descended. There were five of
them. I knew who they were because I recognized Tennison, the head guy. He was maybe a little over fifty, but
tall and lanky, in good shape. He had helped me with a
story when there was a bombing in a St. Paul clothing
store's washroom. One of the things he had explained to
me was that washrooms were the most common places for
bombs to be planted. From my seat on the end of the
couch I watched him take authority easily. He directed
two men in dark suits to the end of the hallway and then
told the receptionist to call someone. But I was too far
away to hear what he was saying. I needed to pull myself
together. I had a job to do.

When I pushed myself off the couch, I felt dizzy. After
standing and letting my head clear for a second, I walked
up to him. I tapped him on the shoulder and he whirled
around impatiently.

"I saw it happen."

"What?" His face changed, tightened. He was listening.

"I was at the end of the hallway when it happened." Flashes of it came to me again. I wished I could sit down, but I held onto the counter I was standing next to.

"What did you see?"

I told him about the young man. "He was holding something in his hand."

"Can you describe it?"

"I actually thought it was a newspaper, rolled up tight."

"Could have been rolled around a pipe bomb. The easiest to make bomb there is. You can stuff them with anything, even matches. At least it helps us know what to look for." He kept clicking the pen he held while he talked. He turned to the doctor standing next to him. "Dr. Evans, I want this place cleared out. Get everyone out of here."

"Sir, we still have some patients in recovery."

"Get them out. We've got to clear the area. There's a very high chance that another bomb is planted someplace. It could go off at any time." He turned to me. "I want you to go down to the hospital and be checked out. I'll send a cop down with you and you can give him a statement."

"I'm fine. Someone already checked me over."

"Right. That's why you're talking so loud. How close to that explosion were you?"

I estimated, then added ten feet. "About forty feet away, I'd say."

"The hallway's not even that long. You were too damn close. I've lost the hearing in one ear. I know what a bomb can do. Now go down and have a doctor look at you."

"Did you have any warning this was going to happen?" I asked him. The reporter in me couldn't stay down.

8

"Listen, Malloy." I was glad he used my last name. It was often the way police dealt with a woman reporter. It didn't bother me and seemed to put them at ease. "This clinic has been threatened with just about everything. But nothing recently, nothing specific. No bomb threats. You got that." He motioned over a uniformed cop. "Take this young lady down to emergency. She's an eyewitness, so get a statement."

I was thinking fast. I didn't have time to go to the hospital. I needed to get this story in by the eleven-thirty deadline to make the afternoon edition. I looked at the cop. He was shorter than me, I was five-ten and I figured him for five-eight and probably a few years younger than me. A rookie. I'd be all right. He took me by the arm, but I gently shook him off.

"I'm just fine, thanks." I was beginning to hear my own voice again.

"I'm Binkley," he said.

"OK, Binkley, lead the way." I followed him outside. A crowd had gathered and was standing on the sidewalk. The receptionist was herding everyone outside. No one seemed to know what to do, yet they didn't want to leave.

"He'll probably cordon off the whole street, don't you think?" I asked Binkley.

"Might."

Lots of information from this guy. He pointed out a cop car behind the ambulance and said, "That's mine."

"Oh, I can't leave my car here. I'll just follow you," I suggested.

"No, I don't think so. I can bring you back here."

Just then I saw the woman who helped me coming out a side door. She was walking with a patient, a woman in her early twenties. The girl was crying and holding her stomach.

"I have to go talk to someone, I'll be right back." I

flew off before he could stop me.

As I got closer, I slowed down. I could see the woman's face and she was younger than I thought. Maybe eighteen or nineteen. She had long brown hair that had been pulled back in a braid, but her hair was so silky and fine some of it had worked its way loose and was hanging in her face. She held a hand over her mouth as if to push the sobs back in, but they came out anyway.

I knew in my gut that this was the girlfriend. Now came the part of my job that I had to force myself to do. It wasn't that I hated it, in fact part of me liked it, and I was kind of ashamed of that. Talking to the grieving relatives. And it was best if it could be done just as they heard the news. They were raw, they were open, they didn't have time to think. The woman left her standing next to the ambulance and went back into the building.

I stepped up and introduced myself. "I'm from the *Times*. It's awful what happened."

"You're from the paper?" The woman hiccupped back a sob as she looked at me. Her eyes were flooded and red.

"Yeah. I just happened to be here. I saw the bomb go off."

"Did you see Bobby?" She was choking down a sob, trying to say more. "What happened to him?"

I pulled my notebook out of the back flap of my purse. I would tell her what she wanted to know, but first she had to tell me a few things. "What's your name?"

"Christine Larsen."

"Christine, what was Bobby's last name?"

"Jameson."

I spelled it back to her. I noticed the cop was starting to come toward us.

"What would you like to know?" I asked. I knew enough to be straight with her. I might not tell her what

10

she wanted to hear, but it would be what she needed to live with.

"Did he really die?"

I could see it in her eyes, the yearning, deep desire to hear it had all been a mistake, even a malicious joke someone had decided to play—anything, anything, rather than the truth. I waited a moment or two and let her eyes fall from my face before I answered. It was too hard to watch the hope get knocked out of them. "Yes. It happened in a flash. I don't think he knew what hit him. If it helps you at all, he died instantly."

"Oh god," she said. "Oh god, oh god." She tried to put her hand in her mouth.

"Listen, Christine. I know this is hard. But I have one more question. Did he want you to have the abortion?"

She sucked in air as the question hit her. I could see she was ready to get mad, the pain was too much. She spit out her words. "Bobby wanted what I wanted. That's what he always said. He loved me. Leave me alone." She turned away from me and leaned her head against the dirty side of the ambulance and cried.

Officer Binkley was next to me. "What're you doing to her?"

"The kid who died was her boyfriend."

I didn't want to leave her so alone. Her head was down and her thin body shook like an aspen tree. I touched her shoulder and said, "I'm sorry. I'm so sorry." Then I looked down at my notebook and turned away. She would have to go through it by herself.

Binkley took my arm and this time I didn't resist. As we walked away he said, "Let's get you to the hospital."

I walked with him to his car and waited while he got in, unlocked the door for me, and started the car. Then I opened the passenger side door and just leaned in. "Listen,

I can't go to the hospital right now, but I will later. I'll check in with Tennison. I gotta go." I slammed the door and started walking toward my car.

Binkley yelled after me, "But I need to get a statement."

"You can read it in the paper," I shouted back, then ran.

3

DRIVING TO THE office, I could feel I was on the verge of hysteria, but I wasn't letting myself tip over into it. Actually there is something about driving that often makes me feel like weeping, but this feeling usually overcomes me on freeways, not dodging down Cretin Avenue, trying to slip through the stoplights. I guess it isn't the driving that does it, but simply that I'm alone and have a chance to think about all that's piling up on me.

I tried to go over in my mind what I needed to do for the story I would write and, at the same time, tried to stay away from the images that wanted to flash across the inside of my forehead like it was a movie screen. And so the bleeding body of the young man was only a blur over the brake lights in front of me.

I have been teased about my emotionality, especially as I am a native-born Minnesotan, coming from a people known for their stoic qualities. As B.T. Hobbs once described the hard-core Germanic stock of this state, "They have feelings that run the gamut from OK to not so good."

The saving grace was that it only took me ten minutes to get to the office from the clinic. I parked my '82 Dodge Dart, a car I had inherited from my mom, in the street, put all the change I had in the meter, and dashed into the building.

B.T. Hobbs was getting off the elevator as I was getting on. He squinted at me through his glasses and said, "What happened to you? You look like a wreck."

"A bomb."

He turned around and got on to the elevator next to me. "I thought you weren't going to go out with anyone for awhile."

"No, a real bomb, B.T." We watched the door close and then looked at each other.

"Shit, you were at the clinic this morning, weren't you?" I could see the lights go on in his thin-slivered eyes. He's a fanatic about a hot story.

"Could you help me, B.T.? Go tell Jack that I've got a front-page exclusive. Tell them to give me about twelve inches."

"Sure. No prob. You were in the building when it happened? Anybody hurt?" He fired off questions like they were bullets.

"I saw it. A guy was blown up."

He shoved his glasses up on his nose. "You're a walking disaster zone. Makes for good stories, but a helluva life." The doors opened on our floor. "I'm off, I'm gone. I'll be by to bug you in a jiffy."

B.T. was four inches shorter than me, and forty pounds heavier, but sometimes I thought we were soul mates. As he moved away from me, I wondered as I often did, how he could make walking look like such extreme physical exertion. He had joined the *Times* shortly after I had, which was six years ago. Before that I had been working on local weekly rags, while he had come from a large Detroit paper.

I went to my cubbyhole and sunk into my chair. Rolling myself up to my desk, I glanced around. Two years

14

ago, the paper had decided to try to give us our own spaces; if you were a regular writer you got your own cubicle made out of prefab walls that went up about six feet. It deadened the noise and unfortunately made the whole floor darker, but we had all grown used to it. In my minimalistic way I had tried to cozy up the gray compartment. There was a wall of postcards, places I could drift into when I needed to get away—a flock of flamingos from Florida, the Casbah in Tangiers, the Pont Neuf in Paris—they crowded the corkboard like broken promises.

In the last few years I had only gotten away once and that was just to the North Shore. It had rained the whole weekend and I had stood on the shore of Lake Superior and watched the waves charge around. Two weeks later I had broken up with the man I had gone up there with and tried to forget the whole weekend and the affair that had precipitated it.

I had to get to the story, but I felt myself resisting it. I didn't know how to handle it. Usually I came to a scene of a crime after it was over, the body often gone, or at least in a body bag. I got the facts, then placed them in the order that would read well. Easy enough. But this time I had been there. It had happened to me. Where was the distance I needed, how could I sum up the explosion into a simple word, how could I compress the sights and sounds into a line or two?

Then it hit me—I had seen someone die today. The moment when the soul gets sucked out of them. But it wasn't for the first time. I looked up at the picture framed on my desk of my mom when she was in her twenties. Soft dark hair like mine hanging loosely to her shoulders. Her eyes gazing off into the distance. Full of wonder, I always thought when I looked at the picture. She had died two years ago at the age of sixty and I had been there with my dad and my brother. She had imploded and was gone.

15

And now I had seen someone explode, the life shoved out of them, splattered across the walls of an empty hallway. I didn't want to write about it. I didn't want to think about it. The pen I held wavered in my hand. I closed my eyes but could feel tears pressing to get out. I leaned my head into the palms of my hands and sat in darkness for a few moments. I couldn't cry right now, there wasn't time. I swallowed the tears and rubbed my hands over my eyes. You can do it later at home, I promised myself. Wait.

I picked up the pen again and worked on the first sentence, which I usually wrote out long hand. It reassured me to see my scrinched up handwriting, reassured me to write a scrawly sentence that only I could read before I turned to the word processor. "A man was killed by a bomb at 9:35 this morning at the Lakewood Family Planning Clinic." Simple, just another story. Except there were at least two groups of people out there—the pro-choice and pro-lifers—who were gearing up to do battle over this issue. I needed to allude to this in the story, but not editorialize.

When I had written the first graph and gotten it into shape, B.T. showed up. He rested his chin on the top of my terminal and stared at me. His head was round and Buddha-like and, piled on top of my terminal screen, looked like the top of a modern-day totem pole. "No, seriously, I've seen you look better," he remarked as if we were in mid-conversation.

I gave him what I hoped was a wan smile. "I need help. I need bolstering, not razzing. Read this." I pointed at the screen.

He came around and stood next to my chair, then leaned over and stared at the screen. "What, the whole first paragraph? What've you been doing all this time?"

"I've been reworking it."

He read it over. I watched his eyes flick over the

screen. "It's fine. It's straightforward. What do you want? It sure doesn't sound like it was written by an eyewitness."

"It's a news story."

"You were there. Put some of yourself in it."

"I don't know if I want to."

He didn't say anything. He stood back and reread the opening. "It's fine."

"I know who the kid was. I talked to his girlfriend. I think I want to do a bigger story. The whole abortion issue is so charged anyway. I feel like I'm weighing every word and I don't have time to do that. I just want to get this out. Does that make sense?"

"Sure, it makes sense." He put a hand on my shoulder. "It was a little rough, huh?"

"He was blown apart. I touched him, but there was nothing anyone could do. He wasn't a human being anymore. How could it happen so fast?"

"Like in the war." B.T. straightened up. "Here comes bustle buns. I told her about the piece. But she wanted to talk to you. I'm leaving. I'll talk to you later."

Glynda Jensen, the features editor, swished up to my side. "What a bit of fabulous luck that you were there. How's it coming?"

"Fine, Glynda. I'll have it done in time for the noon edition."

"Fantastic."

I forced myself to look at her. In many ways I liked her, even admired her. I just wished she wouldn't try so hard. Glynda wore extravagant outfits in purples and reds, often shawls that she tossed around as exclamation marks, and tons of make-up, but she was a good solid writer who had an excellent sense of news. I had worked under her for the last year and she listened to me and usually let me do what I wanted. There were times when I'd suggest a piece and she would veto it, but it happened so infrequently that

17

I listened to her when it did. "I'd like to do a follow-up on this. Do you think Jack will go along with that?" Jack was the news editor. This story was out of her jurisdiction.

"Absolutely."

"I still want to do the feature on the abortion issue, but I'd like to stay with this story for the next week or so. I think I'll get a lot of the information I need for the abortion feature, while working on the bombing incident."

"You've got my go ahead on that."

"Thanks, Glynda."

When she smiled at me, I saw a little of the good witch hidden under her pancake makeup.

I worked on the story for another half an hour and it was coming along. It was dry as B. T. had noted, but it was what I needed to write for the front page. It was eleven o'clock. I had a little more time. I decided to try to get hold of the director of the clinic, Donna Asman. I had seen her speak several times and knew she would not mince her words on this bombing. I had her home number and I thought there might be a chance she would be there.

On the third ring a woman answered the phone, "Yes?"

"Donna Asman?"

"Yes."

I reminded her of our appointment this morning and asked her if she would give me a statement.

Her voice came through loud and clear. "I've been working on that, but you know I'm so angry I can hardly see straight. I just got home. They wouldn't let me stay there any longer. All those women waiting. I had to try to get them into other clinics. I'll be goddamned if this bombing is going to stop what we're doing. Excuse my language. That wasn't my statement. I feel like war has been declared and we are not going to back away. Give me a moment. I wrote something down. Let me get it." I could hear rustling papers at the other end of the line. "We see the bombing that occurred at the clinic as a great tragedy and an unfortunate sign of the unrest caused by the anti-choice movement. The loss of life that happened today at the clinic was an abomination. We, at Lakewood Family Planning Clinic, believe in a woman's right to choice and will open the clinic as soon as it is feasible."

"Any idea when that will be?"

"Lord, I tried to get something out of Tennison, the bomb guy, but he danced all over the place."

"It's hard for him to know." I looked over her statement that I typed right in to my computer, then asked, "It's sounds like you're implying that the anti-choice movement was responsible for this bomb."

"I'm not really saying they are responsible. Certainly, no one knows that yet, but you have to understand what it's like at the clinic. Women, both our clients and staff, are constantly harassed as they enter the clinic. They've been hit, had things thrown at them, been forced to listen to diatribes. Three months ago, a young woman was held hostage in her car by the protestors for about a half an hour before we could get to her. I'm not saying that an organized anti-choice group was behind this, but they have stirred up many people with the rhetoric and I can't help but feel that this is the end result." Donna started out clearly, then her voice broke as she added, "This bombing was our worst fear. I pray they find out who did it."

I thanked her and went back to my story. I shortened her statement, but tried to leave a little of the anger she felt in it. One of my problems in writing this story was I knew more than I should. I couldn't put in any names until they were released by the police. It wouldn't be fair to the family or to the police. If I did I wouldn't get what I needed from either of them in the future. But I kept wondering who this Bobby Jameson was. I looked his name up in the

St. Paul phone book, although he might have lived in Minneapolis. There were several Jamesons, but only one Robert. He lived on Summit. In its heyday, Summit had been the wealthiest street in St. Paul. Circling along the top of the hill overlooking the city, it was lined with elms and huge mansions. Seemed like an awfully ritzy neighborhood for Bobby Jameson. I wondered if he and Christine had been living together.

I had this picture in my mind of him. It seemed to get into me deeper the more I worked on the story. This wasn't just anybody I was writing about, as I had so often done. This story was about a young man I had seen this morning. I had stepped into a hallway and he had turned and looked at me. His dark shaded eyes, his half smile. They made him a real person to me. And I wondered once again, had he been putting the bomb down or had he been picking it up?

4

I⊤ was 8:00 p.m. and Tennison had finally returned from the clinic. I had been calling his office all day and had decided to swing by the Minneapolis Police Station on my way home just on the chance he might be there. The central station was in the old Hennepin County Building, an enormous fortress-like structure made from rough-cut slabs of granite. It was topped with a copper spire, which housed a clock tower. At one time the clock tower could be seen from any place in the downtown area, but now the city had so many obtrusive tall buildings, it was hard to see it from any vantage point. I missed the clock tower when I drove around the city. It had given me a sense of security to see the time posted in the sky, solidly moving forward.

After I had been parked in front of the bondsmen's offices across the street from the station for five minutes, I saw Tennison walk in the main doors of the station. I sat in my car for a few minutes to give him some time alone, then walked past the bronze Father of the Waters in the foyer of the building and down a long narrow hallway to his office.

"I'm sorry for giving your guy the slip," I said when I walked into Tennison's office.

"Don't give me that sorry bullshit." Tennison could

make his voice low and loud at the same time. I was getting the treatment. He leaned back in his chair and looked at me. The desk in front of him was cleared off except for the newspaper, which was rolled up, and I doubted he had had a chance to read it. My article was in the bottom left-hand corner of the front page. "I wanted a statement from you and I still need it. A bomb went off. We've got a dead man down at the morgue."

I could see he was tired. His tie was a little crooked and his hair looked like he had run his hand through it one too many times. It was sticking out funny in the back. He wasn't really yelling at me, but I could tell that he wanted to yell at someone, and I was pretty handy. I stayed quiet. I had learned to do that. Because I planned to stay for awhile, I slid into the blue vinyl chair in front of his desk.

"Tell me what you saw this morning. I gotta understand what went on there."

So I told him all I could remember of walking into the hallway and when I was through and thought I had said everything there was to say, then he started asking me questions.

"He was standing still?"

I stared at the shelves on the wall next to Tennison's desk. Heavy, leather-bound books lined up on the shelves gave an air of authority. When I noticed that the latest "Calvin and Hobbes" cartoon was taped to the edge of one of the shelves, I relaxed. I wanted to get up and look at it, but I closed my eyes and remembered. "He was a little bent over. Then he turned when I pushed through the door."

"How was he holding the newspaper?"

"Kind of cradling it. Not really grabbing hold of it, but letting it sit in his hands. Do you know what I mean?"

He handed me a ruler. "Show me."

I showed him. I let the ruler lay in my hands.

22

"Hmm," he said. "Shit. Are you sure? He wasn't doing anything to it?"

"It's what I seem to remember. Without thinking about it too much. It was only a few seconds before everything blew apart."

"Yeah. It's hard to say."

"Did you find a second bomb?"

"No. No sign of one. Brought in the dogs. Searched the whole building. It's clean."

"Do you think the kid did it? Set the bomb?"

"I'd like to think he did. It would make it simple. We've been trying to find out who else would have access to the hallway. Those folks over there think that place is secure. I'm not so sure."

"How long are you going to keep the clinic closed?"

"As long as it takes. I would guess two to three days. Most of the guys are still over there. I just had to take a breather."

I could picture what the scene at the clinic must look like, because he had shown me when the bomb had exploded at the clothing store. Bomb hunting was like archeology. The bomb squad laid a grid out over the surrounding area. Anything that was found was labeled by where it was found in that grid. They sifted through the dust and debris and identified everything. They worked around the clock until they found all the fragments of the bomb.

"Did you notify the family?" I needed to know. I wanted to move on this story in the morning.

"Yeah, we tracked down the mother of the kid. His name was Robert Jameson."

I didn't tell him I already knew. Just good politics. "What's her name? She live in St. Paul?"

"A suburb. Margaret. I guess the father's dead. But there's lots of siblings. I just talked to her on the phone. We had the girlfriend ID him at the scene."

I winced, thinking of how awful that must have been for Christine. But hopefully they had covered the body and just let her see his face.

"I'm going to stay on this story," I told him.

"I figured. If you want anything more from me, you better get your butt in here tomorrow morning and give that statement to someone. I'm too tired to do anything more with it tonight. But I wanted to ask you those questions."

"OK." I stood up.

"Did you get your ears checked out?"

"Yeah, I did. I went to my own clinic. They said I was fine." My doctor had fit me in between two appointments. I hadn't even called, just gone down there. He peered into my ear with a light and said it might take a day or two for all my hearing to come back. He had thought I should be tested in a month or so.

"Good," he said absently.

I waited for a moment to see if he had anything else to say. Often I learned the most at the end of an interview when I stopped asking questions. When I let go of what I think I want to hear, then people often tell me amazing things. They finally tell me what they need to say. But Tennison looked done in, so I turned to go.

I heard his chair creak behind me and then he asked, "Malloy, did I ever tell you you remind me of my daughter?"

I stopped and faced him again. He wasn't looking at me. He was staring at the wall. "No."

"Not a lot." He shook his head. "But there's something that's the same. Maybe the eyes. She's off at college. Haven't seen her in a while."

"She must be younger than me."

He laughed. "Yeah, I suppose a lot younger. What're you, all of thirty?"

24

Thirty-five, I thought to myself as I left.

* * *

I stopped off at the co-op and picked up some fast health food. Tofu in a box. Then headed home.

I lived in the Seward neighborhood of south Minneapolis. In the sixties and seventies, all the hippies, most of the druggies, and a good share of the artists and musicians, claimed the West Bank of the Mississippi as their haven. I had lived there for quite a while. But as they aged and wanted a bit more security, many of them moved to the next closest real neighborhood, Seward. It offered more houses, fewer apartments, and they bought the old homes and planted gardens in the backyards. It was a colorful neighborhood, not a particularly safe one, but I liked it.

Four years ago, I had moved into the upper floor of a duplex and had even done a few things to make it more mine. The duplex was a classic thirties dwelling. Hundreds of them had been built in south Minneapolis during that period. Brick and stucco on the outside. Handsome woodwork throughout. Usually built-in buffets in the dining room and small built-in bookshelves in the living room. I painted my bedroom a soft pale yellow so it looked like the sun was shining in even when it wasn't. Just a trick that made it a little easier for me to get up in the morning and god knows I needed every trick. And I put up faded lace curtains to let the light come in.

I climbed up the stairs and before I put down anything I was carrying or took off my coat, I looked across the living room and saw that the little red light was glowing on my answering machine. A small blessing. Someone had thought of me. I dumped everything on the couch and re-wound the machine. Then I played the messages back as I took off my coat.

One hang-up. Drat. A message from my father. Un-

25

usual. He hardly ever called me. Probably because he knew I'd call him at least once a week. Since my mother's death I was keeping an eye on him. He had slowed down a lot in the last few years and lived all by himself. "Laura, this is your father. Just wondering if you're coming down this weekend. Nothing special." There was a long pause and then he hung up. I'd call him in the morning. He lived an hour and a half away in Waseca and I usually visited him every couple weeks. I don't know if he was aware that the same road I took down to see him could bring him up to Minneapolis.

Then came a voice that I hadn't heard in a month and that I didn't want to hear and, at the same time, wanted to hear desperately and my blood started running the wrong way through my veins.

"Yeah, I know. I'm not supposed to be doing this. Laura, I hoped I would catch you in. It's about nine-fifteen. I wanted to talk. Give me a call. Gary."

I looked at my watch—nine-twenty. I just missed him. He just missed me. Shit, that's what our whole relationship had been about. Had been. Remember, past tense. There were no more messages so I reached down and rewound the machine. Caught the tail end of my dad's message, "nothing special," and then I heard Gary's voice again. I closed my eyes. He sounded the same, but he didn't sound like he was suffering much. Hard to tell though, he was good at covering up. His wife had never guessed a thing. Or so he told me.

I had always liked his voice. I rewound the machine and played his message one more time. It had been such a pleasure to come home and listen to a message from him. The sound of his voice was like chocolate, rich and dark and made me get a little hot. I missed him.

I sat down on the floor and leaned my head against the table leg. Tears leaked out of my eyes. They had been piling up there all day long and once they started coming out, there was no stopping them. I cried for the sad me that missed Gary and the scared me that almost got blown up today and the tired me that wanted to feel someone's arms and, most of all, for the adult me that wouldn't call him back. I went into one of my deep cries and dug out all the reasons the tears should keep flowing, a well of tears: my mom's death, my dad's loneliness. When I ran out of personal sufferings, I moved on to the world. AIDS killing babies and otters caught in the oil spills. The otters always got to me, I could picture them so clearly just swimming along like they had done all their lives and then this black, smelly, gluey stuff would get in their eyes and noses, cover their bodies and they would drown. I had to pull out of this tailspin.

I grabbed the table leg and stood up, then rewound the tape. With a flick of my finger, I erased it. I wouldn't call him. I couldn't start it up again. It had shredded me to stop seeing him, but I was through the worst of it, I told myself. Yet I couldn't help wondering why he had called.

There was someone who needed some attention, so I walked through the house and came to the hallway closet. I opened the door and peeked in. A little white bundle was curled up in a large blue wool sock. I saw two eyes blink open, and then the pile of fur unfurled and stretched. My ferret yawned and started to slide toward me. Then she got her feet under her and ran up to my feet. Her name was Fabiola and she had been named after the Queen of Belgium as I thought she had rather a regal air about her.

"Hi, you little scoundrel. Have you been getting into lots of trouble? Trying to break out of your room? Digging underground tunnels through the plaster?" I held her up to my face and she licked my cheek. Remnants of tears with their salty trace were a real treat for her.

I draped her long thin body over my arm and we went

into the kitchen so I could start boiling the tofu delight. "Yes, your favorite. White food. You always think anything that's the same color as you is the best. Don't you."

While the meal cooked, I leaned against the sink and stared at the kitchen. It was the only room in the house that was a little cluttery. But I liked it that way. Cookbooks lined up under shelves. Pots of rosemary and lemon geranium and other herbs on the shelf under the window. I tried to remember to water them when I took my vitamins in the morning. Two banks of wooden cupboards that had miraculously escaped the paintbrush and shone with a glow that only sixty years of sunlight could give them. A jazz singer friend's latest poster magnetized to my refrigerator. A small wooden table where I ate most of my meals was pushed up against a wall. This was the room I spent most of my waking time in when I was home.

Twenty minutes later we sat down to a healthy but tasteless plate of tofu au gratin. Fabiola had a nibble or two but then tried to slither down my leg, so I put her on the linoleum floor. She hopped over to the radiator and slid underneath it. She loved small, dark places.

As I ate I thought about the articles I wanted to write. There could be a big story in the bombing incident and I wanted to follow it. I always wrote best when I wrote about someone, when I had a person to focus on. I needed to find out who Bobby Jameson had been. But, at the same time, I didn't want the abortion feature to be dropped. Glynda had been hesitant when I suggested it. She didn't want to stir up trouble and at the same time she did. That's how newspapers were sold after all. But she certainly didn't want the pro-lifers to boycott the paper. So we had had a long talk and agreed to keep the tone of the piece extraordinarily neutral. I knew this would be tough for me. In fact, I always had to work hard to keep my voice out of my work.

I had been raised by a mother who was extremely liberal. Her best friend in college had died of gangrene after an illegal abortion and my mother had cried with happiness when the Roe v. Wade decision came down from the Supreme Court. I would have to work extra hard to have the pro-lifer's side heard in this piece.

As I was setting my plate in the sink, the phone rang. The dishes from three days were stacked up there, almost time to wash them. I looked at my watch again. It was ten o'clock. The phone rang again. I knew it wasn't my dad. Growing up in farm country, sundown saw him thinking about bed. I started to walk towards the living room. The brrring of the phone was louder. My ears were back to normal. Shit. I didn't want it to be Gary. But I didn't want to be afraid to answer the phone in my own home. Standing in front of the phone, I let it ring one more time.

I picked up the receiver and held it to my ear, but didn't say anything. I had seen someone do that in a movie. I waited and the caller didn't say anything either. I thought that was weird. So I made my voice kind of rough and said, "Yeah?"

"Laura, are you all right?"

"B. T., why didn't you say anything?"

"That isn't how it works, Laura. See I call, the phone rings, you pick it up and say 'hello.' Do you want to try it again?"

"No."

"Maybe just take it from 'hello.'"

I laughed. "OK, hello."

"What a day, huh?"

"Yup, it was some day." I stood up and started walking through the dining room with the cordless phone. I had bought it recently and was still reveling in the freedom. I often walked through my house while on the phone, simply because I could.

"You feel like going to get a drink?"

I thought. B. T. and I did this once or twice a week. We'd meet at some dive and have a beer or two and analyze the world situation, both at the newspaper and in the macrocosm. It usually did me good, let me unwind, stay sane. "I don't feel like it tonight."

In the silence that followed I felt like I could hear him thinking. When he was done, he asked, "Have you talked to Gary recently, like tonight?"

"Not exactly." I sat down at the kitchen table.

"OK, explain that one to me."

"He left a message on my machine."

"And now you have to stay home and wallow." He made it a statement so I would have to refute it.

"I know it's going to seem like that, but if you recall I just about blew apart today." I stopped for emphasis, then went on, "And all I want to do now is climb into bed. Maybe even sleep."

"I get it. Don't blame you. Did you get ahold of Tennison?"

"Yeah, he didn't have much for me. Nothing I didn't know. But he's leaving the channels open. I was worried he might shut down on me. I did pull a fast one today."

"Yeah, but you're cute. You can get away with things like that. Now if I would have tried that I'd be in jail."

"Is that a sexist comment?"

"Possibly. Hey, the article looked good. Well, sleep well. Give that frisky little ferret a good shaking for me."

"Night," I said and hung up.

I didn't seem to be able to move. Holding my head in my hands, I stared at the patterned tablecloth under my elbows. The way the red petals of the flowers swirled around the yellow centers. Fascinating. I had never really noticed it before. I jumped when I felt a scratching on my ankle. The beast was making her presence known.

30

I hoisted up Fabiola and went to do my toiletries—all the washing and brushing that I needed to do to be sanitized for bed.

I put Fabiola in the bathtub so she couldn't go and hide on me and then stared at myself in the mirror. Dark thick eyebrows, which I liked, but I wished my hazel eyes were bigger. Shoulder length auburn hair that was starting to flip at the ends. Time for a trim. Then I made myself smile and looked at the consequences. A pattern of wrinkles. Curved lines plucked up the corners of my mouth and accented the bottom of my eyes. This was my animate face and I had come to appreciate it. There was a life story in those lines. They were the markings of loves and worries and sorrows and pleasures. The only wrinkle I disliked was the one between my eyebrows. I smoothed at it, but knew it was on my face too often during the day. When I thought deeply about something, I literally furrowed my brow and that wrinkle was the empty furrow. I flared my nostrils, then ducked my face to wash it.

In my bedroom I picked up off the floor a big old T-shirt saved from one of my former relationships, and pulled it on. Flannel sheets were on the bed and I sighed as I slid into them.

I reached down and lifted Fabiola up off the floor and she immediately burrowed under the covers. I decided it was one of the nights when I would let Fab sleep with me. It didn't happen very often, because she liked to get up at six o'clock and in order to wake me up, would lick my eyelids. But I decided I needed the small spot of warmth she would provide. I needed to know I was not alone.

5

I COULD TELL spring was coming because I could catch smells in the air again, a hint of green, of growing. The snow was almost gone, left only in scanty piles in the darkest shadows alongside houses. My car was parked in front of Mrs. Margaret Jameson's residence in Maplewood, a suburb of St. Paul, and I was readying myself to go in and talk with her. I had never lived in the suburbs and it was a place I didn't understand—rows of houses all the same. Not really the community of a small town, and certainly none of the culture of the city. But the ring of suburbs around the Twin Cities was growing, according to the demographers.

The dark green house looked familiar to me because so many of them had been built in the fifties. A small two-story house with a breezeway that connected it to the garage. When I reached the end of the driveway, I had to decide which door I would walk toward. There was a door in the breezeway that I was sure led into the kitchen and I was also sure this was the door that everyone in the family and their intimates used. But since I wasn't a member of this group I headed for the front door that went into the living room. I pushed the doorbell, heard it ring in the depth of the house, and waited.

I had called ahead and Mrs. Jameson had agreed to see me. Her voice was thin but clear on the phone. She had hesitated before she said yes, but that made me feel she was smart—after thinking a moment, she knew the story had to come out and figured she might as well be the one to do the telling. But maybe I read too much into her pause.

When she came to the door I was surprised by her appearance. She was much older than I had imagined. Her hair was completely white and her face was finely wrinkled, especially around the mouth, where the thin lines formed a smoker's pucker.

After opening the door, she looked blankly at me for a moment and then shook her head. "Come in. You must be the reporter. I can't seem to keep things in my mind." Reaching out to me, she gave my hand a one-beat shake.

"Mrs. Jameson, it's good of you to give me this time. I just want to say I'm so sorry about your son." I hadn't told her over the phone that I had been a witness to his death and I hadn't decided if I would tell her.

"Yes, yes," she said softly while backing into the living room. It was a dark, cozy room. There were more pictures on the wall than any decorator would have allowed, mostly photos, but they were all ordered and straight. A big maroon couch stood against the wall facing the picture window and an afghan was tossed at the foot of it as if someone had been lying under it and then risen in a hurry. In the corner next to the couch was an old-fashioned black woodstove with a brick floor built around it.

She fluttered her hands at the room. "I haven't been able to do a thing. I was just lying down. Felt kind of cold all of a sudden. Come in to the kitchen."

"Thank you," I murmured as I followed her again.

There was a hallway with a door that I assumed went upstairs and then a combined dining room-kitchen area. A long oak table took up most of the space and there were five or six dirty coffee cups on it. Behind the table was another large window, this one overlooking the backyard. A bird feeder dangled off a pole not many yards away and a squirrel jumped off it as we sat down at the table. I slipped out of my coat and took a pen from my purse.

"He wouldn't do it," Mrs. Jameson told me. "Bobby would never do such a thing." She said it gently and quietly as if she were teaching a young child a hard lesson and wanted to be clear about it.

I didn't say anything, but let her go on.

"Don't get me wrong, he wasn't perfect." She stopped and wiped at an eye. "In fact when I think of him, that's what I've been remembering, all his shenanigans. What a culprit he could be. But he never did anything meanly. That's what you have to know. He didn't have a mean bone in his body. Why, he even hated firecrackers."

I thought I'd start easy, with questions I actually knew the answers to. "He was twenty-two, wasn't he, Mrs. Jameson?" I pulled out my notebook and placed it on the table, not wanting to make a big deal about it. Often people were surprised I didn't use a tape recorder, but I wasn't good mechanically and I felt more comfortable writing down the answers.

"Born July third. Always upset about that. When he was older he'd tease me, couldn't you have waited a day, Ma? And right here in St. Paul at St. Joseph's Hospital. He was the baby of the family." She sat with her hands pressed together, her first fingers under her nose and her thumbs under her chin. Her eyes unfocused slightly as she talked. "And you don't need to call me Mrs. Jameson. Everybody calls me Meg. It's all I'm used to."

"OK, Meg." I tried to say it easily. I found it hard to address an older woman who I didn't know by her first name, but I always used a first name in an interview if I could. The more personal the conversation could be, the more I would find out. "How many children in the family?"

"Hard to think there are only four now. There were five. My son Paul is the oldest. He's thirty-three. Then there's the three girls—Bridget, Maddy, and Kathleen. Bridget and Maddy were here this morning. Kathleen lives in New York. She's a lawyer. The smartest of the bunch. She's flying out tonight."

"And Paul?"

She shut her eyes, tightly pressed them closed as if she were in pain. "He's taking it real hard. He doesn't quite know what to do. I know he's blaming himself. I can see it. He and Bobby were very close. After my husband died, see he died when Bobby was only ten, then Paul kind of stepped in." She rubbed her eyes, then opened them and looked at me to see if I was taking in what she was saying. "He thinks there's something he could have done that would have prevented all of this. Last night he was drinking and I didn't like the looks of it, but I didn't say anything. I think that's what the drink's for—so you can drown a little and cry."

I nodded to her and wrote for a moment or two.

"You won't write anything about him drinking, will you?" she asked after a gentle intake of breath.

"No, of course not. I'm just jotting down the names of your children. Was Bobby going to school or did he work?"

"A little of both. He was trying to go to school every once in awhile, but Paul would let him work at his store when he needed some money. He owns the Tinder Box."

I thought, vaguely remembered the name. "Over by Snelling?"

35

"Yes, not too far from here. He sells woodstoves."
She sounded proud. "Did you notice the one in the living
room?"

"Yes."

"Paul gave it to me for Christmas the first year he
owned the store. I love it. There's nothing like a fire on a
cold evening." She rubbed her hands together. "I haven't
even offered you something to drink. I'm really not myself. Would you like a cup of tea?"

"I would love one." I usually preferred coffee, but tea
sounded good to me. "Do you know Christine, Bobby's
girlfriend?" I was starting to move into the questions that
really mattered.

She filled a stainless steel, well-used tea kettle with water and put it on a burner. "Of course I knew Christine.
She and Bobby had been going out for nearly three years
now. She's a good kid. They met in high school."

"Did they live together?"

"Yes. I didn't really approve, but Bobby told me everyone does it. I guess I knew that everyone did it, but it's
hard when it's your own kid."

"Did you know Christine was pregnant?"

Meg walked to the large window and looked out at the
backyard. "When my husband was alive he would flood
the garden in the winter and all the neighborhood children
would come over and skate on our rink."

"Meg, did you know?"

"No, I didn't." Turning to look at me, she grabbed the
back of a chair. For the first time I heard anger in her
voice. She continued, "I wish I had. I wish I could have
talked to the two of them. I'm Catholic and as you know
the church considers abortion a sin, but more than that,
that child was my grandchild. I don't have one yet. My
daughters are doing their careers and all that. I'm not getting any younger. I'd have loved to have had a grandchild.

None of this would have happened. Bobby'd be alive. God, I wish he were alive. I'd give anything." At the end of her speech her voice quavered and she wrapped her hands around her belly and rocked herself. "The killing and the waste of it all I can hardly bear."

"I'm sorry," I murmured, seeing her try for composure and not gain it. The tears glistened on her face, but she made no crying sounds, she just rocked. I waited for her to come through it.

There is a fine line between taking advantage of someone's distress and trying to get the story, and I think the line is different for each writer. But I felt something in my gut when I pushed too hard at a vulnerable moment, and when I felt this slight twinge of disgust I pulled back and waited. Everyone deserved respect and I would only take what they wanted to give me, which didn't mean I wouldn't ask hard questions, even questions they didn't want to answer. All they had to do was say, "No, I won't tell you." I tried never to assume what someone would or would not tell me.

I heard a door bang and then a tall, dark-haired man stepped into the kitchen from the breezeway. He took a look at Meg, who was still crying silently, and then at me and asked, "What's going on here?" His voice was low and resonant, almost gruff, like he had a slight cold.

He turned his eyes on me again and asked, "Who are you? Mom, what's happening?"

I was caught by this man. He was taller than me, actually by several inches, and had on a dark brown bomber jacket, unzipped, with a soft blue workshirt on underneath. He had blue eyes, and black curly hair, soft curls that would form ringlets if they were allowed to grow. I was sure his mother would have said he should have been to the barber's as his hair in back hung over his collar.

I was just about to say something when Meg calmed

down and pointed at me. "Paul, this is a reporter from the *Times*, Laura Malloy. She's just asking a few questions. I'm blubbering away like I do. It's not her fault."

"A reporter, what the hell? Mom, you don't need to do this. What has she asked you?"

Meg unwound her arms from around her waist and stood taller. "I do too need to do this. You know they think Bobby set that bomb and there is no way he did. That policeman was asking all those questions and I just didn't get the feeling he listened to what I was trying to tell him." Meg turned back to me. "You know, Bobby wasn't the kind of kid that stood out. He was no scholar and he didn't play sports. He was an average kid, but he had a gentle heart. When he was little he would bring home baby birds that had fallen from their nests and feed them with an eyedropper. Do you remember, Paul?"

"Sure, Mom." He came up and put his hands on her shoulders.

"He cried easier than most boys, now maybe he got that from me, but still and all, he would never hurt anyone."

"Do you think he would have wanted Christine to have the abortion?" I asked my last important question.

I saw Paul stiffen and Meg just shook her head. "I would hope not, but I don't know. I just don't know. He didn't talk to me. I'm not sure how he felt about all that. Maybe then . . . "

I made a decision then not to ask Paul what he knew. I didn't think he would talk easily in front of his mother. He was protecting her and I liked him for that. Just then the tea kettle whistled and we all jumped.

"I'm making some tea, Paul, would you like some?"
"Sure."

I stood up and put my coat on. "I should go. I'll have to take a raincheck on the tea. I have another appointment.

I want to thank you for your time. If I need to ask you more questions, may I call you?"

"Of course. Oh, and I wanted to give you something." She walked with me into the living room and Paul followed. She pulled out the drawer of an end table next to the couch. After rummaging around, she found what she was looking for and handed it to me. I recognized it as a picture of Bobby from the brief moment I had seen him.

"It's his graduation picture. See, you can tell he's a nice boy. Look at that smile."

She was right. The most one could say was that he looked mischievous. His dark eyes were squinted into a smile and his full lips curved open, revealing white straight teeth. Two dimples and a smattering of freckles softened his slightly angular face. But I knew you couldn't tell from a picture, you couldn't even tell from a face. Sociopaths were charming. They had smiles that broke your heart. I had interviewed a number of them and had even considering writing to a guy in prison, but when I found out that he had murdered his wife by "accidently" running her over, I had changed my mind.

"He was good-looking," I told her.

"Yes," she sighed, and continued, "yes, he was." I could tell she was about to start crying again so I shook her hand, thanked her and turned to go.

"I'll walk you out," Paul said.

When we got outside I told him, "You're going to be getting more media people. I'm just the beginning. That bomb is news. You've got two major groups up in arms about it. The pro-lifers and the pro-choice people. They're not going to let this die down."

"Shit. I suppose you're right." We were standing on the front step and he reached into his pocket and handed me a card. "Listen, Miss Malone."

I interrupted, "It's Ms. Malloy."

"Sorry. Anyway Ms. Malloy, don't call my mom again. This is too hard on her. If you have any more questions, you can always reach me at my store." Then he turned and went inside.

I sat in my car and let it idle. I wondered what Paul knew and why he didn't want me to talk his mother anymore. Probably he was just taking care of her. I looked at his card, "The Tinder Box." Meg had said Bobby worked at the store. He must have had access to tools and pipe and matches there.

Thinking of the fairy tale about the tinder box I shook my head, but then I remembered that the phrase was also used to describe a highly flammable person or situation. I might have to pay Paul a visit at his store, I thought as I pulled away from the Jameson house.

6

WE GOT IT for the view, we got it for the address. Summit Avenue, la-de-da. It's a stupid little one-bedroom apartment, but we could see the river." Christine was sitting on a futon bed-couch in front of the window that framed the view, but she was looking at me.

Out the window I could see downtown St. Paul, the High Bridge, and the Mississippi River. The bluffs of the river were a soft misty green from the newly budding trees that covered them. Bobby and Christine's apartment was in an old house that had been broken into odd little spaces. The apartment was actually two big rooms: one was the living room, dining room, kitchen and the other the bedroom, which had a bath off of it. But the view out the window caught the tops of the trees and a glimpse of the city down below.

"Just think, if I was pregnant now, I couldn't smoke a cigarette." She lifted the one she held in her hand and inhaled and blew the smoke out in a steady stream.

I had expected Christine to be a mess, but she wasn't. She had even remembered me from yesterday when she answered the door and said, "I thought I might see you again." It surprised me because she could have so easily said that in a mean way, but she only sounded bemused.

"I could sit here all day and not talk to anyone and I

41

probably would have if you hadn't come over." She blew out another stream of smoke and then stared at it. She was wearing a man's flannel shirt, I guessed it was Bobby's, jeans, and thongs. One thong dangled off the end of her foot and she kept clicking it up against her heel. "This friend of mine gave me a few tranqs. Last night I told her I just had to sleep. If I get thrown I can't sleep and I hate that. It makes everything go around in a circle. The next day is worse, I'm more anxious and then I really can't sleep. So, anyways, she said here and gave me a handful of pills. I took one last night and felt like I was sleeping on a cloud. Have you ever taken a tranquilizer?"

"No. Just codeine."

"That's a pain killer, right? Not the same at all. This makes you drifty and you just don't care. When I think about Bobby I cry sometimes and they're like pretend tears, like a sprinkler system."

"Tell me a little about Bobby." I nudged her in the direction she was headed.

Christine tossed her long brown hair back. Today it was hanging down loose and looked as if she hadn't washed it. "That'll probably get the old tears streaming. Tell you about Bobby. God, I've known him all my life. We went to grade school together. He was three years older than me, but we rode the same bus. He was friends with my brother. It was in junior high that I really noticed him though. I thought he was so cute. He had a shag haircut that was pretty long in back. But we didn't start going out until toward the end of high school. I snagged him. I really went after him." She stopped, remembering.

She twisted her hair around her hand and then plopped the bun she had formed on the back of her neck. As she talked the shank of hair unwound and slid down her back. "I asked him out. Can you believe it? I just didn't think he'd get around to it. As soon as I did though, he took over." She smiled and got out another cigarette. "I asked him out and through this weird chain of events he's dead. So I guess it's my fault." Her voice was getting dreamy like she was talking in her sleep.

"So what was he like?" I prodded her, seeing that she could drift off on me.

"Pretty funny, real smart, but kinda lazy." She put the cigarette back in the package, which took her a few moments of concentration. "I don't really want to smoke, but my hands seem to want to. Bobby. He just wasn't too motivated about things. I think he figured Paul would take care of him. And there was some truth in that. Paul would always give him a job, so Bobby never had to look for one. I don't think he ever knew what he wanted to be."

"I talked to Paul and he said Bobby worked around the shop for him. Was he handy?"

"What do you mean?"

"Could he fix things—like a radio, a TV?"

She crumpled her chin. "Sure, but not anything special. He knew how to use a few tools. His brother Paul taught him how to install woodstoves. I guess he was all right at it."

She looked at me more closely, her large brown eyes narrowed and I stared right back at her. "You're leading up to something, aren't you? Why don't you just ask me outright what you want to know? You didn't have any trouble yesterday." With this last sentence she picked up a plate that was sitting on the coffee table and had the dry crust of a sandwich formed into a C. She poked the crust with her finger as if she were trying to see if it were still alive. When it didn't move, she snapped it in two and nibbled on the piece that was left in her hand. "What do you want to know?"

Again she wasn't saying any of this meanly, more matter of fact. I appreciated it. "You're right. That was a leading question. See, I do want to get to know who Bobby Jameson was. He's going to be real important to me for the next week or two. I have to try to convey to our readers who this young man was. But, to be blunt, which you don't seem to mind, I'm trying to see if he had the expertise to build a bomb."

Christine leaned forward and burst out of her stupor. "I don't get this. Why would anyone think Bobby would want to blow the place up? The cop was nosing around about that. Isn't it obvious who set the bomb? Those stupid people that parade around in front of the building, screaming in your face when you try to walk by them." Then she deflated, collapsing back on the couch. "I hate them."

Again I waited. She hadn't answered the question I had asked, but I needed to give her a little time to calm down and come around to it. "They are pretty disturbing people. I'm sure it wasn't pleasant for you to have to deal with them on your way into the clinic."

"This one woman got right in my face. What does she know about what I went through." Christine held her hand right in front of her own face to show me how close the woman had been and then tapped herself on the nose. "Free choice, that's the basis of our country, isn't it?"

"To a certain extent." I drew a little American flag in my notes, then said, "I'm still curious if you think Bobby could have made a bomb."

"Sure, he could build a bomb. Bobby wasn't dumb. But I just don't see why he would. He's not opinionated about anything. He usually doesn't care one way or the other. I got the impression that he hadn't even given the abortion much thought."

"You did talk about it, didn't you?"

"Yes, but I did all the talking. He just listened. Bobby was so good-looking, when we first started going out I'd just stare at him. But he was quiet. Sometimes I'd ask him a question and it would be a minute or two before he'd answer. So when I told him I was pregnant and told him I wanted an abortion, he didn't say anything right away. Then he said he'd like to go with me when I had it."

"Why did you want an abortion?" I felt on shaky ground asking her this question. It seemed as personal as they got. But I wanted to understand what had gone down between the two of them.

Christine thought for a moment. I could tell she was thinking because her eyes were more focused and she was biting on her upper lip. I glanced around the apartment. There was the bare minimum of furniture in it—a table with two folding chairs, the futon couch and a small TV in the large room. From where I was sitting I could see into the bedroom and saw that their bed had been just a mattress thrown on the floor. A notebook was lying open on the bed and I wondered what Christine had written in it. I had the urge to snoop, to open drawers, peek behind things. I wanted to know what the inside of their life together had been like.

Christine waved her arms around and laughed. "Where would we put a kid? We didn't have the room here. I'm only nineteen years old and I'm not a romantic. Bobby was a goof and I'm waitressing. We have a good time together, but I didn't want to get married and I didn't want to start a family. Getting pregnant was a mistake and I wanted to fix it." She rattled her statement off pretty fast. It sounded as if she had been asking herself the same question and had been trying to convince herself of the answer.

Then she laughed, a short bitter laugh. Her voice got husky and she went on, "Lookit. I had a mom who didn't want me. She tried hard, but she was too young and she got pushed around too hard by my dad before he skipped out on us. All I know is what a mom shouldn't be. I didn't

45

want to be like that. I didn't want to be trapped and hate my kid and hate my boyfriend. Do you get that?"

"Yeah. I get it."

"You see, I want to go to college. Nobody in my family did, but I know I could cut it. I did well in high school. I just gotta get the money together. I know I can do it."

I thought she could do it too. She was awfully articulate for a nineteen-year-old. "I'm sure you can."

She gave me a stare, then asked, "What do you think about abortions? You ever have one?"

Once in awhile the questions were turned on me and when they were I tried to answer them honestly so I could expect the same in return. But I didn't want what I thought to get in the way of an interview. It was a fine line. However, I wanted to support Christine and I thought she had made a good decision for where she was in her life. "I absolutely think they should be available. I don't know if I'd have one at my age, but that's my personal decision right now. So far I haven't needed an abortion and I feel lucky."

"Yeah, it is about luck. When I found out I was pregnant I was pissed. I refuse to be on the pill anymore. It makes me bloated. Bobby hated rubbers. I could only persuade him to wear one if I said I was really fertile. I was sure I was safe and that's when it happened. You slip up once and that's all it takes."

"What did Bobby have with him when you went to the clinic? Was he carrying anything?"

"Well, he always has a backpack with him. I never pay attention to what he stuffs in it, books, magazines. He's always reading. He likes these weird fantasy books with monsters and gargoyles on the cover or something."

"Did he read the newspaper much?"

"I don't know. If it's lying around." She rested her head back on the couch and shut her eyes. She was a big, healthy girl, but there was a fragile look around her eyes, a hint of blue from the fine veins just under the skin. She looked like she could use some sleep.

"How did Bobby seem yesterday? Did you notice anything unusual about him?"

"Like I said it's kinda hard to tell with Bobby 'cause he's so quiet. The only thing I remember that struck me funny was that he gave me a big hug and told me everything would be all right. That was just as I was going in for the abortion. I thought it was real sweet of him. I'm glad he did it. That was the last time I saw him."

I could see she was starting to tear up and I decided I had questioned her enough for now. "Thanks, Christine, I'll be in touch." I stood up and handed her my card. "Please call me if you think of anything."

She stood up and took my card. At that moment, her eyes were vacant, but I had seen them drift in and out of awareness. The tranquilizer would keep her zoned, but the right question or a strong memory would pull her up out of that sea of soft oblivion, and then her eyes would clear and be slick with pain.

I couldn't help it, I was worried about her. "Have you talked to your mom about this?"

Christine shrugged her shoulders. "Nah. She's living down in Florida these days. We don't talk much."

"Will you get together with the Jamesons?"

"I talked to Meg. She asked me to come over there, but I don't want to. I just don't want to face them right now. I know they're going to blame me."

I didn't want to argue with her about that. I wasn't so sure she wasn't right. After meeting Paul and Meg Jameson, I could picture the family closing up against her. "Well, you take care of yourself."

Christine nodded her head and then as I watched her I saw her eyes widen and her face flinch. "I can't believe this. Why?" She didn't phrase it as a question, but rather a lament. She stuffed her hands in the pockets of her jeans and shrugged her shoulders. "It's weird. If I was still pregnant now, Bobby'd be here and you wouldn't."

7

THE STREET was dead empty and it was the middle of a weekday. The sun was glaring off the windows of the buildings, the wind was blowing the just-budding tree branches, but there were no cars. I had parked back by the barricades and was walking down the center of the street. Lakewood Avenue was deserted like a movie set that wasn't being used, when it was usually one of the busiest streets in St. Paul.

When I buzzed at the door of the clinic, a uniformed policeman opened the door and stepped aside when I showed my I.D. card. The waiting room chairs had been moved all to one side of the room and on the other side a long table had been set up that had bags of plaster and little bits of wood on it. No one seemed to be around and I wondered if they had all gone to lunch. My stomach rumbled at the thought.

The door to the hallway had been removed and was propped up against the wall in the waiting room. Walking around the table, I came to the end of the hallway and was surprised by how little trace there was of what had happened. Bobby Jameson's body had borne the brunt of the explosion. The hallway wall right where he stood had been damaged, the windows had blown out, but structurally everything seemed sound.

When someone tapped me on the shoulder, I let out a holler that scared him as much as he had scared me. "I'm sorry," I said quickly and when I turned I found myself staring at a pair of close-set dark brown eyes.

"Goddamn, so am I," the cop said abashedly. "Can I help you?"

"You working with Tennison?" I asked.

"Yeah, you want to see him?"

"No, actually I was told that Ms. Asman was here today in her office. I would like to talk to her."

"I'll show you the way."

We walked down the hall and I remembered the last time I tried to get to her office, but let it only flicker through my mind.

Donna Asman looked up at me from her desk as I introduced myself and waved a hand at a chair. "They say we've got to keep the clinic closed another two days. This is ridiculous. I was hoping to open tomorrow. The longer we're closed, the more I feel like we're losing the war. Don't quote me. God, I have a big mouth. Sit down. You're tall. Have you got heels on?"

I showed her my comfortable loafers.

After another glance up at me, she kept her eyes down, writing away at something. "Always wished I was tall. Then I could eat more."

"It's nice of you to take the time to talk to me."

"Oh, come on. You're the press. I gotta talk to the press. Have a donut." She pointed at the white paper bag perched on the end of her desk. "I brought a bunch for the guys, but they didn't eat as many as I thought they would. If they sit there I'll eat them all. Help me out."

"Thanks." I reached in and pulled out a sugared donut.

"Give me a second here," she said and continued writing away at something. I was glad to. I needed to eat this

50

donut as somehow lunch had passed me by. When I was on a story I ate on the run, but the run could get pretty long and hard and not necessarily go past anything nutritious. This donut would keep me until I got back to the office.

I had seen Donna Asman once or twice before, but had never realized how small she was. Seeing her sit up straight behind her desk, I guessed she was barely over five feet. In her mid-fifties, she had a big personality and a large voice. I had heard her called the "little boulder" by both her enemies and her friends. Her hair was a brassy blond that nature would never bother to copy, her eyebrows two slanted dark bird's wings, her lips covered with a peach color that matched the sweater she was wearing, but didn't help her complexion. But her dark brown eyes were large and caring and her voice had a gravel tone that bespoke the miles it had come and would go to help you out. She was a motherly person. I knew she had two natural children and two adopted and a husband who stood silently behind her. I think he sold life insurance.

She signed whatever she was working on, I assumed it was a letter, and pushed it away. "I won't let anyone else come in to work, but I filled out some kind of waiver for myself. Just don't feel right being away from here too long. I guess we're lucky that the damage was so minimal, but every time I think of that kid I just want to cry. What would make him do such a thing?"

"You think he did it?"

"This is off the record. I will give you a few quotes that are on the record, but I have a horrible feeling it was him. But I wish to god it was that guy who runs Lifeline. I haven't seen him in front for a week or two now, but his wife is out there everyday. I've heard he's traveling now, going to different towns and stirring up support for his cause. Have you ever talked to him?"

"I've heard him speak, but I've never done a one-to-one with him."

"Slimey as they come. He could wriggle through a needle hole. I don't understand why he's so convincing to some people. I guess they just like to hear their own evil thoughts spoken out loud."

"Have you ever had a run-in with him?"

"No, and that's been very purposeful. I have to keep this place running. I'll do just about anything to keep it running and I can't afford an altercation with that man. I'm as civil to him as I can possibly be and I instruct my staff to be the same. Those Lifeliners are bad enough traipsing up and down the sidewalk, we don't need to get them riled up."

"Have there ever been any violent acts here before?"

She looked up at the ceiling. "Give me a moment. I've got to switch into my public mode here. We've been relatively lucky at this clinic up until now, no one has been hurt. I think you and I talked about this yesterday. I had so hoped we would not have to deal with all this."

"How long have you been the director here?"

She smiled. "I've been the director for the last five years, but I worked my way up the ranks. I started work here when the clinic opened, nearly twelve years ago. I was a counselor then, doing pregnancy counseling, working mainly with teens. Clinics like this are needed now more than ever. Our teenage pregancy problem is growing by leaps and bounds. And it's not the low-income girls we see in here—it's the suburban, middle-class white teenager. See, one thing that a lot of people don't know is that in 1900, the average age for menstruation was sixteen and the age a guy could support a family was sixteen. Now the average age of commencement of menstruation is eleven and a half and the age a woman and a man can support a family is twenty-five."

"Wow." I remembered the day I got my period—I was in sixth grade and was sure that everyone could see the pad I was wearing through my clothes. It felt as big as a diaper.

"Yeah, this problem is real. Girls can get pregnant thirteen and a half years before they would be able to provide for that baby. Oh, don't get me started."

"No, this information is just what I need." I explained how I was working on two pieces at once.

I got the information about when the clinic would be officially open and then she said, "I wish you could play this whole thing down."

I didn't say anything. We both knew I couldn't.

"It's just so hard trying to keep an atmosphere that's conducive to working here at the clinic. I know my staff is very shook up about this latest event. I'm sure they're all thinking it could have been one of them. I don't know if you're aware of what's been going on around the country, but clinic workers have gotten quite a lot of abuse. They've been hit by cars and even taken hostage. One woman was punched by a protester in New York state when she was pregnant and miscarried as a result. It's been tough."

"How does your husband deal with this?"

"Roger offers to come and walk me into work about once a week. I always turn down the offer, but I know he means it. He stays out of this, but he lets me know he's behind me one hundred percent. He takes the kids a lot more than me. I'm lucky."

I nodded my head. Watching the way her face opened as she spoke of her husband, I thought she was darn lucky.

"You ever let people look at articles before they come out?" she asked.

"No, I don't. It's the *Times* policy not to and there

really wouldn't be time in most instances."

"I just wondered."

* * *

When I climbed back in my car, I tried not to look too closely at it. About once a month I weeded it out, but since I spent more time in it than I did at home, it always had a very lived in look: bags from Wuollet's bakery, lots of old newspapers that I tried to recycle, and tapes in and out of their covers from constant use. I aimed the Dart back toward work. I needed to put in an appearance at the office. To come flying through and look very busy, reassure everyone, plus I needed to check to see if anyone had called. I had one more interview to do and then I could call it a day.

The business and editoral office of the *Twin Cities Times* were on University Avenue, quite close to the dividing point between Minneapolis and St. Paul. The building, which had been built in the fifties, was actually in St. Paul, but the paper claimed it was located where the two cities joined. Just as the Mississippi River meandered through the two towns, the *Times* was to be literally an integral part of them both.

There was a rivalry between St. Paul and Minneapolis. The St. Paulites saw themselves as a more solid crew. Their city was the state capital, the town had grown slowly and was much more careful to preserve its lovely old buildings. While Minneapolitans, with all the tall buildings, claimed to be more sophisticated, more "looking to the future." I thought the melting snow-pile of the "Hump" Dome and the tinker-toy Target Center, both sports arenas, were two of the ugliest bookends the city planners could have chosen, but I liked living in south Minneapolis.

I took the time to park out back in the long-term

cheapo parking lot and then took a little more time to notice the green sprouts of the tulips that were planted alongside the building.

Instead of going straight to my desk, I went to find B.T. His desk looked like he was around—there was an opened and unfinished box of Cracker Jacks near his computer—something he would never have left behind. His computer was on, although that was a sign of nothing. B.T. felt that the computer was an extension of his brain and its rhythmic humming was as essential to him as breathing. He often left it running around the clock and told me again and again it was actually better for computers than switching them on and off.

So I figured he was close by and I guessed he was probably hiding out in the coffee shop. I headed off to find him and to have some sort of lunch. A clock on the wall said it was three.

The coffee shop had three booths and four long lunchroom tables in it. The food was edible and warm and inexpensive and the soups were always homemade. That just about did it for me. I saw B.T. sitting in the back booth poring over something.

The first thing B.T. said to me as I walked up on him, without even lifting his eyes from the *Utne Reader* he was perusing was, "They got some flak on your story."

I was busy looking around for Darlene the waitress. "How could that be? That was the most obsequious news piece I've ever turned out."

"Talk to Glynda."

"Do I have to? Maybe I can just avoid her today."

"Talk to Glynda." He finally looked up and bugged his eyes out at me. It was his way of underlining his words. That's what I really liked about B.T. He never worried about what people thought about him, or what he looked like. He'd get his point across any way he could, so I had never bothered to tell him that when he bugged his eyes out he looked even more like Don Rickles than usual.

"She's having a bird, isn't she? She's threatening to pull me off the story. Never print another word about a bomb blast that killed one person." I was just guessing at the worst that could happen. Never hurt to be prepared.

"Actually that's not what she's worried about. I think it's you." He turned a page of the *Reader*.

"What's me?" I grabbed the magazine away from him so he would pay attention to me.

"It's you she's worried about."

"Oh, no, this is serious. That could really put a crimp in things. Is she going to play mother hen with me?"

"May-be." He made it sound like it was two words.

"Do you know what the flak was all about?"

"Rumor has it it was a threatening fax."

"God, technology can be so misused."

Darlene came and stood quietly to see if we had anything to say to her. She rarely butted in to a conversation. Sometimes B.T. would ask her a question, to see if she could talk. But she usually slipped by with just a nod. I smiled at her and said, "I'd like a BLT and a bowl of whatever kind of soup you have and a Dr. Pepper."

"How can you order a soup and not even know what it is?" B.T. burst in. "What if it's something you hate?"

"What, like tripe soup?" B.T. always picked on me when I ordered. I could never do it right for him. Usually I didn't pay any attention, but I was cranky and hungry.

"Could be lima bean soup," he suggested. Those round, dry, little mouth-sucking pale green slug-like beans were one of the few things I hated and B.T. knew that.

"Yugh." I looked up at the waitress and she nodded her head no so I felt safe.

After she left I asked him, "What did it say?"

"Glynda wouldn't tell me, so my guess is it's bad. She was kind of shaking with indignation like she wouldn't even condescend to repeat what it said. My guess is it's threatening to the paper or to an individual who works at the paper. Hurry up and eat so I can find out."

"I might just sneak out."

"Don't you dare."

"I want to talk to the Lifeline people today."

"What if it's them?"

"Do you think? Didn't you interview their leader, Tom Chasen, once? What's he like?"

"Perhaps you'd like to come back up to the office and look at my notes."

"Just tell me." Darlene managed to slide in my food around my notebook, which I got out to jot a few questions down. I noticed that the soup was clam chowder, one of my favorites.

"Chasen is a middle-aged guy, about forty I think. He's got a pretty weird past. He used to play guitar and was in a couple bands that fizzled out." B.T. folded his pudgy hands and rested his head on them. "I think he's always wanted to be on stage about something and now he's found his cause. He made a living as a salesman before forming Lifeline, but now I think he's making his money solely from his lectures and such. He's married, his wife is very active in the group, she might be who got him going in it, and they live in Edina."

"You're kidding." I was surprised to hear they lived in the richest suburb of the Twin Cities, actually of the five-state region: the Dakotas, Iowa, Wisconsin and Minnesota. "He must be pulling in some dough from this."

"I guess, they're right across the border. A half a block off of France, but still it's Edina."

"So what's your take on him?" I asked as I crushed

two crackers together in their cellophane package and then ripped it open and poured them over the soup.

"He's not real smart, but he's got a kind of people sense that's uncanny. He dresses conservatively, but preppy. He wants to come off as establishment, but he's not. There is something underneath him that is way off-center. I think he's got a thing about women and I have a feeling he's not too fond of children. Ironic, isn't it?"

"How could you tell that?"

"Just a feeling. He wouldn't hardly let me say a word to his wife. He kept shepherding her into the kitchen or upstairs."

"What's her name?"

He rubbed his temples with his hands, then looked up at me. "I don't quite remember. Cindy maybe."

"You never forget a name."

"She's mousy, stayed way in the background."

I made a note to myself to be sure and talk to her. She might be kept in the background for a reason. I offered B.T. half of my BLT and he scarfed it down. I knew he would, he had been eyeballing it. Darlene brought the check and we both threw in some money.

"I'm not going back to the office," I told him as we left the coffee shop.

B.T. stopped and demanded, "What about me?"

"What about you?" I looked down at him.

"I need to know what's on that fax so I can get on with my work." He looked up at me, batting his short stubby eyelashes.

"You'll get it out of Glynda if it's that important to you."

"I'll walk you to the lot. Get some air."

"Back to Chasen. Do you think he could be violent? What's his plan of action?"

58

"Oh, yeah," B.T. said without hesitation. "He talks in codes, but he paints the picture like all these men, because it's mostly men who are in the front line with him, are in a war to save the children. And in this war, violence would be permissible."

8

I TRIED TO REACH Tom Chasen at the Lifeliner's office, but they said he was out for the day. So I took a chance and called his home and talked to his wife. She was soft-spoken and rather nasal on the phone, but assured me he would be home by five o'clock and would be glad to take time for me. As I hung up the phone, I wondered why he would be glad to talk to me. But then as I got thinking about it, I realized he must see it all, every interview, as just more publicity for his cause.

I got there about fifteen minutes early. I often did that. Then I could case the joint. I didn't have to do a last-minute rush and feel out of breath when I started the interview. As I parked my car in front of an average-sized rambler, probably circa 1970, I saw someone crouched down on the front lawn. I got out of my car and walked toward the person. As I got closer I saw it was a woman and she was digging in a bed of dirt.

"Isn't it a little early to be preparing a garden?" I asked.

She turned her head with a thin smile on her face. It looked to be as much as she could manage. "I won't plant anything for several weeks yet, but I just like the feel of the dirt. I'm anxious to get going. I'm going to plant snapdragons and marigolds and petunias. A huge bed of flowers."

Fairly traditional stuff, I thought, as I had recognized all the names. "Sounds lovely."

"Do you garden?" she asked me, as she squatted back on her haunches.

"A little." I stretched the truth, thinking about the few herbs I had perched in my kitchen.

"I just like to see things grow. I always have." She had a claw-like instrument in her hand and pulled it through the dirt a few more times, then stood up and brushed off her knees. "I'm Sandy Chasen."

"Hi, Sandy, I called earlier. My name is Laura Malloy."

Her face shut down slightly like a cloud had passed overhead. "Oh, you're the reporter. My husband isn't here yet. Let me take you inside."

"I know I am early, but I got done with my previous appointment sooner than I thought."

When Sandy stood, I noticed that she was about average height, around five-five, shoulder-length brown hair pulled back in a clip. She seemed familiar to me, but I couldn't place where I had seen her. The very large glasses she wore made her small eyes look like dots in her face. She had crosses in her earlobes and the only other piece of jewelry was a plain gold wedding band, which she obviously hadn't removed to garden. She was wearing a plaid short-sleeved shirt and blue polyester pants that had an elastic band at the waist, not an attractive ensemble, but then maybe it was her gardening outfit.

She led me into the house, asked me to have a seat in the living room. When she kept going, I assumed she was heading into the kitchen. The living room was decorated in new Early Americana. A couch upholstered in a rustic rusty tweed was placed under the picture window, a rocking chair with a sneaky looking eagle carved into the top of it sat across from the couch, and a wagon wheel leaned up

61

by the fireplace, but I was sure nothing in the room was more than fifteen years old. After a few minutes passed, I began to suspect that Sandy wasn't going to come back into the living room, so I went after her.

"Could I have a drink of water?"

"Oh, where are my manners? We have iced tea and some juice. Would you like something like that?"

"I'd love a glass of iced tea. Drinking that and seeing you garden will let me believe summer's really on its way."

She gave an odd little giggle as she opened the refrigerator. I was standing behind her and got a glance at the inside of it. Everything was lined up in rows, by size. She actually used the egg tray for eggs, something I had never seen anyone do. So much orderliness gave me the willies, but didn't surprise me. The house was spotless, at least the two rooms I had seen so far. But it went further than that. There was nothing out on any surface. The counters were clear, not a book, a coffee cup, a salt shaker. Nothing in the sink. No yellow slips posted to remind them of anything. So little evidence of life.

Sandy held out a glass of iced tea for me. "Do you take anything with it—sugar, lemon?"

"No, thanks, this is fine." She watched me as I took a sip. It tasted like home-brewed. "This is delicious."

"I make it fresh every morning. It's Constant Comment."

She took homemaking to new levels of perfection. I was trying to think of a way to move the conversation around to something besides gardening and tea-making when she commented, "I like your pin."

I looked down at the dancing woman. It was a pin that my mother had worn a lot. Inexpensive costume jewelry but nicely done. The woman looked Persian and her arms and legs were held at odd angles so I assumed she was dancing. "Thanks. It's kind of a good luck charm for me."

"I wear one too." Sandy pulled out an amulet that she had on a chain around her throat. It wasn't particularly attractive, a little lumpy bag. I stared at it and didn't know what to say.

As I looked up at Sandy's face for an instant I imagined doing a make-over on her. I had always loved the makeovers in *Seventeen* magazine when I was a teenager. I'd cut her hair into a bob, pluck her eyebrows, give her contacts, fill out her lips with a soft rose color, fit quarter-sized gold hoops in her ears, dress her in a cream-colored blouse with the sleeves rolled up and well-worn jeans. She would be a different woman—she'd leave dishes in her sink, offer me a gin and tonic, complain about her husband's lovemaking.

"It's a fertility bag."

I snapped out of my reverie at the word "fertility" and asked the logical question, "Oh, are you trying to get pregnant?"

Her hand wrapped around the gray little bag until I couldn't see any of it. She hung on to it and pulled it back and forth. "We've been trying for years." She gave a brilliant, frightening smile and said, "But I'm sure it'll happen again soon. The Lord will give us a baby. Sarah had one when she was ninety years old."

I wondered who Sarah was, but was afraid to ask.

Sandy stood still and closed her eyes. "It says in the Bible, Genesis 17, verse 16: 'I will bless her, and moreover I will give you a son by her; I will bless her, and she shall be a mother of nations; kings of peoples shall come from her.'"

I was glad I hadn't revealed my ignorance. "Have you seen a doctor?"

"Yes, and he said I'm healthy and fine. So it's in the Lord's hands."

"And your husband?"

"Tom doesn't need to see a doctor. He's had a vision of many babies. He said they will come as a reward for all the ones he's saved."

I wondered what his sperm count was, but didn't think Sandy would have a clue. Just then the front door slammed and a male voice yelled, "Is she here?"

Sandy's shoulders hunched and she motioned me out of the kitchen with her head. "Yes. She just got here. I gave her some tea, because she was thirsty."

As I stepped into the hallway, I saw Tom Chasen for the first time up close. He was young and very business-like, carrying an attaché case and a newspaper.

"That was nice, dear." He patted her on the shoulder and slightly pushed her back into the kitchen, while motioning me to follow him into the living room. I stopped and turned back to Sandy.

"Thanks for the tea. I hope your garden blooms well this year."

She ducked her head and turned away from us without saying a word. He had her well trained.

I decided to sit in the eagle-backed rocking chair and Tom took off his suit coat and relaxed on the tweedy couch. "I've had a hard day. I hope you don't mind if I get a little more comfortable."

I gave him what I hoped was an amiable smile and said, "Of course not." I watched him get comfortable, which involved loosening his tie and slouching a bit on the couch. He wore aviator wire-rimmed glasses, a style that had been popular in the mid-seventies. His blond hair was wispy and he fluffed it with his fingers.

"So how do you feel about babies being killed?" he asked me.

"I beg your pardon." The bluntness of the question sent me scrambling.

"Where do you stand on the abortion issue? I've had trouble with the press about this."

I opened up my notebook and pretended to be checking over something before I looked up at him. "I'm a reporter. We don't take stands on public issues. It would get in the way of our work."

"Yes, but you personally must feel one way or the other."

"Whatever way I feel will not get in the way of my telling the story that needs to be told. I appreciate your concern, but I'm really here to find out your response to a bombing that occurred in St. Paul yesterday. Did you hear about it?"

He spread his lips, but didn't open his mouth. The facial grimace resembled a smile except it didn't seem to express joy in any way, rather a kind of smugness. "Oh, yes. My lines of communication work extraordinarily fast. I probably knew about it before you."

I didn't think that was possible but I have learned not to contradict the people I interview. Then I wondered if it could be true, if he had known about the bombing before it happened. "When did you hear about it?"

He seemed to pull back in. "Well, it was in the morning sometime. I'm not exactly sure when."

"Do you think there is a chance that one of your people had something to do with it? The bomb?"

"The lives of children are at stake. Every day between ten and twenty children are killed in that clinic alone. In the Twin Cities, there are in the hundreds and in the state of Minnesota, close to fifteen thousand a year. Why should there be such a fuss about this young man who brought his girlfriend down to get an abortion? He was very much involved in the killing of young innocent blood that took place yesterday. The scripture is clear on what revenge can be taken."

The last thing I wanted to do was start him quoting scripture at me. It just didn't work in the paper. "It does sound like you are in very close contact with the people in your group." He nodded affirmatively and I went on, "So I just wondered if there had been any rumors or whatever that someone from the Lifeliners had something to do with the bomb?"

"This is difficult to talk about because I cannot condone such behavior. But as you know it is a very emotional cause. We cannot stand by and watch women take the lives of our children. We must stop them any way we can."

I felt like I was swimming around in rhetoric soup. I could not get a straight answer out of him. "I'm confused . . ."

Before I could go on, he broke in, "You are?"

I waited to see if he was done, then went on, "Yes, Mr. Chasen, I have read about your group. I do understand what you stand for and I agree with you it's a very emotional issue." He smiled at this. "But I'm trying to find out if, to your knowledge, your organization had any connection with this bombing?"

He stretched out his legs, pursed his lips and plucked at them with his thumb and forefinger. I gathered it was his pensive posture. I waited and hoped for some semblance of a straight answer. "Actually I've been checking into that myself. I'm not sure that there is a connection. And I'm not sure that if there were I would tell you of it."

That was as straight as it got. "Do you have the names of any of the Lifeliners who were there that day protesting?"

His eyes flickered toward the kitchen, then back to me.

"Was your wife there?" I asked.

"It's possible." He drew out the two words as if anything were possible.

I remembered that Sandy had seemed familiar to me when I had first seen her. Maybe I had noticed her as I went into the clinic yesterday. "Could I talk to Sandy again before I go?"

He stood up. "One thing that is sacred to my wife and I is our time alone together. Sandy is making dinner right now and we will be eating shortly. I'm sure you understand how important it is for us to protect our private life."

"Yes, of course I do." I stood up, but tried again. "I'll get in touch with Sandy some other time when it's more convenient."

He reached out and shook my hand. "That's fine, although she's quite busy these days. She is an enormous help to me in my work, but she feels her place is in the background and might not want to speak with you."

I didn't argue with him and I didn't bother to give him my card. I knew he would not call me if he heard anything. B.T. was right. This guy did not like or trust women. Even his own wife.

9

I WAS PULLING my keys out of my purse when a man stepped out of the shadows from around the side of my house. His footstep thudded on the sidewalk and his dark form showed up against the light stucco of the neighboring building. I was ready to blow the whistle I had attached to my key chain when I recognized the man as Gary.

"What the hell?" I said.

There he stood, all six-feet-one of him. He didn't have his hat on, but other than that he was dressed in his full police uniform. I wondered if he was on duty.

"God, who did you think I was, a rapist?" he asked. His deep voice had a roll of authority to it. He had been on the St. Paul force for fifteen years.

I couldn't see his face very well in the dark, but I could hear the laughter in his voice. "What are you doing here?"

"You didn't call me back. I was worried about you."

"Yeah, and do you think there might have been a reason for that lack of response on my part? That it could have been a deliberate decision?"

"You always get so mouthy when you're mad." He smiled up at me, still standing on the sidewalk below. "Can I come in?"

I turned and faced the door, sliding the key in the lock.

He was here and I wasn't going to get rid of him easily. Maybe we needed to talk once more. Things between us had ended pretty fuzzily. The door swung open and I said, "Just for a minute. OK?"

"Yeah, right."

He followed me in the door and up the stairs. I was conscious of him walking behind me, that he was probably looking at my legs. He had always liked my legs, comparing them to those of many racing animals—gazelles, greyhounds, thoroughbreds. He'd run his hand up the inside of my leg, feeling the bone, stroking the muscle. Yup, my legs had not been the problem in our relationship.

At the top of the stairs I turned on the overhead light in the living room. No mood lighting for this conversation. Instead of heading toward the couch, where I usually flopped, I sat in the rocking chair next to it. Gary perched on the edge of the couch and stared at me with a hesitant smile.

He wasn't good-looking, I thought to myself. He was big, close to overweight, and his face was craggy and pockmarked. Walnut brown hair fell in a hank over his forehead. But when he smiled, it was all you could look at. He even got dimples in his cheeks and his eyes turned into thick, brown lines. As I returned his look, he smiled a full-powered smile at me and I admitted inside my heart that I was glad to see him.

"You look good," he said. "How're you doing?"

I had been running around all day and hadn't had a chance to look at myself in a mirror. I pulled off my big brown and black suit coat that I wore over almost everything I owned. It was a man's suit coat and had inside pockets, in which I stashed pens and notebooks.

"I'm fine," I said, raising my shoulders.

"I'm glad to hear that. Heard about the bomb and all and I wanted to check in with you."

"What did you hear?"

"That you witnessed it. That Tennison was pissed at you."

"He's not anymore. We talked."

"Good. I don't know—when I heard you came that close. . . . I'm having a hard time with this, with not seeing you."

"Yeah, I know." I couldn't say much more.

"It's not a big deal, maybe we could get together once in a while. I could stop by. We could keep it real casual."

"I thought we already did casual." When Gary and I had first met, I had thought an affair with him would be the perfect set-up. I didn't want to get seriously involved with anyone, but I was ready to have a man in my life. I met Gary through another police officer I knew from working on the crime beat and he seemed like the answer.

He leaned toward me and touched my wrist, then wrapped his broad fingers around it. "I miss you."

"That's nice to hear." I kept looking down at his hand.

"Well, what's the point of all this? What are you trying to do?"

"The point is we didn't make it. It wasn't enough for me." I remembered the night I came up against it. I thought I was pregnant because my period was a few days late and I felt completely alone, even more so than if I had been seeing no one. I couldn't call Gary at home and I certainly didn't know what we would do if I was pregnant. Even after I got my period, I hadn't been able to tell him about my scare. I realized I couldn't keep seeing him.

"What if I told you I was thinking of separating from Anne?"

Anne, the mysterious wife I had never met, I wondered if she knew what Gary was up to on his late-night shifts. "I wouldn't believe you."

"You're so fucking smart. Come here." He pulled me

70

toward him and put his arms around my waist as I stood in front of him. "All I want is to be with you."

I could feel every atom in my body wanting him, but I also knew this was our thing. We liked the tragedy of it, we played on it and it was not healthy. I enjoyed wanting someone I couldn't have.

I leaned in and wrapped my arms around him, resting my chin on his shoulder. I had liked the rendezvous after work in bars, in squad cars. It gave me a thrill to have him come over to my house and slide out of his uniform for a fast hour. It meant I didn't have to wake up with him in the morning. We didn't go grocery shopping together. There were days when we didn't see each other, didn't even talk. When we got together, we didn't talk over our daily lives. Face it, we didn't do much talking at all. But he smelled good to me. The way I remembered.

The doorbell rang. The chimes for the doorbell were in the kitchen and it had been broken since before I moved in. The sound it produced was like the death rattle of an old horse.

Gary pushed me off his lap and jumped up, looking for a wild moment like he was going to pull his gun. "That's not that damn ferret making that noise, is it?"

I started to giggle. "Ferrets don't make any noise. It's the doorbell."

"Are you going to answer it?" he asked.

"Yes, I live here. I'm going to answer it." I turned and ran down the stairs before I could change my mind. Halfway down I could see the top of an old Twins baseball cap, the one where the two baseball players have their arms wrapped around each other's shoulders as they stand on each side of the Mississippi. Since the head that it was on barely reached the bottom of the door window and since I knew only one person who had that rare hat and would still wear it, I guessed that B.T. had stopped by.

71

When I pulled open the wooden inner door, B.T. pulled open the outside screen door, and started talking: "I brought over a copy of the fax. I persuaded Glynda to let me see it and I can understand now why she's so upset. And I brought over my file on Tom Chasen."

"Great. Do you want to come in?" I backed up the stairs.

B.T. looked around the front entryway, then down at the grocery bag he was holding. "I am in. I also brought a couple brewskies and a bag of your faves—Cheetos."

"The way to a girl's heart." I moved up a couple more steps, then made a decision. "Well, Gary's here, but he was just leaving."

"Oh." B.T. stopped. "I could just drop these things off. I don't have to come in."

"No, come on."

Gary appeared at the top of the stairs. "Hi, B.T." Gary knew that B.T. knew what had gone on between us. I had explained early on in our affair that B.T. was my closest friend and that I had to be able to confide in someone.

"Gary, made any interesting arrests lately?" B.T. asked.

"Nothing newsworthy."

We all stood awkwardly at the top of the stairs, then B.T. said in his chummy voice, "Yeah, well, I'll pull out some of this stuff..." and walked toward the kitchen.

When he was out of range, Gary put an arm next to me on the wall and leaned in close. "So you don't want to see me anymore?"

"Right." I raised my head up and looked him in the face when I said it. He wasn't smiling and his eyes were as wide open as I'd ever seen them.

"OK, I get it but I don't believe it. You know what I mean?"

"Yeah, I do. I know."

He stood there for a moment more. He was deciding something and when he didn't lean down and kiss me I knew what he had decided. This would be it. When he walked down the stairs, I wrapped my arms around my body so I would have something to hold on to. He closed the door quietly behind him and I tilted back against the wall. Tears gathered around the edges of my eyes, but didn't leak out. I blinked a couple times and listened to B.T. slamming around in my kitchen. I guessed he was trying to make a lot of noise so we wouldn't feel like he was listening in. I was glad I had some work to do.

When I walked into the kitchen, B.T. had it all laid out. There was a big red Fiestaware bowl full of bright orange cheese puffs, two Leinenkugel beers uncapped, a ripped-open envelope and a thick file folder spread out on the table. "You might as well look at this and really feel bad about everything in the world." He handed me the envelope.

"This is a copy of the fax?"

"Yeah."

"How'd you get a copy from Glynda?"

"The usual amount of threats and wheedling."

I pulled a sheet of paper out of the envelope and unfolded it. It was a picture of a fetus with its eyes closed, its head thrown back, its tiny hands clenched. There was a gun held to its head. Underneath it were the words: "There was more than one person killed at the Lakewood Clinic Monday morning. Write the truth about abortions or the killing will continue."

"Yuck," I said.

"I know it's yuck. What gets me is it's also news and I don't think we can touch it."

"Did Glynda contact the police?"

"Oh, yeah. She went right to work on this."

"Did they trace the fax?"

"They did. It came from a copy place on University."

"That's right by the Lifeliner offices," I said when I figured out where he meant.

"I know."

"That could mean nothing, or that somebody's trying to set them up, or that they are pretty stupid."

"Probably one of the three." He took a swig of beer and I followed suit.

I turned the fax over, not wanting the image of the fetus to float in front of me any more.

"How's Gary?" B.T. asked as he started to rifle through the Chasen file.

"Seems fine."

"What'd he want?"

"To persuade me he's not fine."

"And how are you?"

"Definitely not fine, but I'll survive."

"Have an orange squishy thing." B.T. lifted the bowl of Cheetos and held it out in front of me.

"Don't mind if I do." I grabbed a handful and munched my way through them.

"OK, I looked through this file before I brought it over and it's interesting. I don't know if anyone will ever do this guy's biography, but he's taken some sharp turns in his day. Did you know he was married once before?"

"No. Really?"

"Yeah, to a woman who now runs a flower shop, but was quite a radical."

"Did they have any kids?" I thought back to my conversation with Sandy Chasen and wondered if she would ever get the baby she wanted.

"No, no children. They weren't married very long. They met during an anti-war demonstration at the University of Minnesota." B.T. shoved the file at me, then asked, "What exactly are you looking for?"

"I'm not sure. I want to understand how Tom Chasen came to be who he is, I guess. I'm certainly going to need to go into his point of view for the abortion piece. But I also have a feeling he knows more than he's telling about the bombing."

"Wouldn't surprise me. The Lifeliners' network is quite extensive and very well organized. Do you think they had something to do with the bombing?"

I thought back to when the bomb had gone off and told him what had been bothering me. "If Bobby Jameson set the bomb, then why didn't he do it before Christine had the abortion? It doesn't make sense that he would wait."

"Interesting question."

"B.T., one thing I'm worried about in writing this abortion piece is how can I be objective about this. How do you handle it when you have to interview someone and you can't stand what they're saying?"

"I've got this trick. I pretend that we're on TV and the whole world is watching us. And I'm like Johnny Carson, you know, a nice guy who's just trying to find out what's on their mind. B.T. has to go away for awhile. Then when I leave the interview, I rehash it in my mind, saying everything I wanted to."

"I've been doing a lot of thinking about the pro-lifers. What would you do if you actually believed that life started at conception and that babies were being murdered?"

B.T. held his beer bottle by the neck and tried to make it spin around. It wasn't often he stopped to think about an issue. I waited for him to answer. Finally, after another swallow of beer, he said, "I'd hand out condoms in high schools."

10

I LEANED BACK, read the last sentence, and typed a period on to its end: "Police are still investigating the blast, but the clinic has reopened." The story wouldn't run on the first page, but might make page one of the metro section.

I had tried to get through to Tennison that morning, but he hadn't returned my call and when I checked around with my other police sources I learned nothing new. The body was still at the coroner's, fragments of the bomb had been sifted out of the debris and it did look like it was a pipe bomb, but there was no statement as yet from the bomb squad. So I rehashed what I knew—I didn't want to let the story die.

I closed my eyes and heard the room hum around me. It was the busiest time of the day—right before noon—deadlines galore. B.T. had popped in but didn't stop long as he was working on a column about the city council meeting. He really enjoyed going to the meetings, said it was the best gossip he got all week. B.T.'s column ran in the metro section every other day. It was always funny, usually biting, and filled with weird information. There was a small picture of him in which his smirk was visible.

Swiveling away from my terminal, I grabbed the edge of my desk and pulled myself up to it. In the middle of my desk sat my list for the day and I was pleased to cross out the first item—"Write continuing clinic story." Paul Jameson had called earlier and we set up a meeting at his store. He had been vague about why we were meeting and I guessed that he had as many questions to ask me as I had to ask him. There was still a guardedness about him, and I wondered if it was simply his nature.

Also on my list was—"check out Tom Chasen's ex-wife." I wanted to know what he had been like before he had taken up his crusade against abortion. He sounded like he had been more of a liberal, bordering on radical. What had changed him so much?

But next on my list was my meeting with Glynda. Her office was just down the hall from my cubicle. As the features special projects editor, she had an office with a door and a room with a window. But then she also had to stay in the building most of the day, so I thought that was fair.

Her door was ajar but I gave a rap and walked in. Glynda was bent over her desk with her reading glasses perched on the end of her nose. She was wearing a full peasant skirt of burgundy and gold, a gold sweater and a pair of black riding boots. I wondered what fictitious character she thought she was today. "B.T. gave you the fax, didn't he?"

"Yes, ma'am, he sure did." I reached into my folder and pulled it out. There was something so inherently disturbing about the picture, the rock metal of the gun held against the fragile eggshell-like skin of the fetus that I didn't want it within easy eyesight. "He said they found out where it came from. Any leads on who sent it?"

"No, I don't think we're going to find out. You don't need to show I.D. or anything to send a fax. And at those copy places they don't look at the faxes, so they really don't have any idea who sent it." She sounded so subdued I looked at her closely. Her face didn't have much color. Maybe she had scurried through her make-up routine faster than usual this morning, or maybe she was too pale under what she had applied. Glynda, for all her splash, was actually a very private person: she had married in her late thirties and had no children. Now, at forty-five, she had the job she wanted and worked hard.

"Glynda, are you all right?"

"I'm fine. It's just that. . . ." She pointed at the fax and read the statement on it, "'Tell the truth about abortions or the killing will continue.' You know that caption can be read two ways—as a threat or just as a statement that abortions will continue."

"Yeah, I thought of that."

"So what are you doing for me today? I'd like to have an idea of where you're going with this big story."

"The more I think about it, the more I see myself working on two separate stories. I still want to do an overview of the abortion issue. Remember that's why I went the clinic in the first place. I see this bomb going off as making it more timely. And I want to continue putting out the follow-up stories to the bombing. I think the information I collect for the first story might end up having some relevance in the second."

"Overview of the abortion issue, does it make sense for you to write that now?"

"More than ever. I think most newspapers are avoiding it because they think it's a loaded gun." I couldn't help glancing at the fax. I wrinkled my nose at my slip. "Just because there's no easy answer to the abortion issue doesn't mean it should be ignored."

"When am I going to start to see some of this?"

"By the end of the week, I hope."

"I've been told to keep a close watch on this piece. Jack wants the lawyers to go over it when it's done. You understand." Glynda wasn't looking at me. But I did understand. Then she pulled her glasses off her nose and her eyes landed on me full force. "Be careful, Laura. People are all wrought up about this issue."

* * *

The Tinder Box was right off the freeway, and as I exited I could see the building, but I couldn't figure out how to get there. Finally I found the frontage road and pulled up in front of the brick building.

I adjusted the mirror so I could get a quick look at myself. I pulled a pair of silver dangling earrings out of the inside pocket of my blazer and stuck them on my ears. I rubbed at my cheeks to give them a little color and smoothed my eyebrows into place. After giving myself a scrunchy smile, I got out of my car. Before going into the store, I walked up to the side yard and stared.

Wood was piled a cord high, all along the side of the building and then for what seemed to be a good acre behind the building. What a beautiful form of energy, I thought. I knew it wasn't environmentally correct these days, but seeing all that firewood made me feel warm in the same way staring at a mink coat did.

When I walked into the store, I understood why all the wood was piled behind the building. There were about five fires blazing in wood stoves scattered around the room. I wandered through the store, admiring the good assortment of stoves they carried: contemporary-looking Jotuls from Sweden, Waterfords from Ireland with a country scene molded on the side of the ceramic stove, traditional black-sided stoves with open grills. There were rocking chairs and easy chairs set in front of many of them so you could sit down and enjoy them while you tried to decide which would fit in your rec room.

After a quick tour, I went to the counter and told the

older woman behind it that I was there to see Paul Jameson.

"Oh, can I help you?" she asked as if she hadn't heard what I'd said.

"I'm here to see Paul. I have an appointment."

"There must be a mistake. He's seeing a newspaper reporter any minute now," she told me conspiratorially.

"I know," I whispered back. "I'm the newspaper reporter."

"My heavens." The woman pushed at her blue-white hair and then looked at me accusingly. "He shouldn't even be here, the shape he's in. He came down just to meet with you. You be kind to him." She stared at me and I nodded my head. "OK, I'll tell him you're here." She pressed on an intercom and I heard a faint buzz sounding in the depths of the space. "He's in his office in the warehouse behind there." She waved her hand at the back wall of stoves.

I looked the direction she waved and saw Paul Jameson step around a partition. He was still tall and walked like he was out in a field, loose and full, like he owned everything around him, which I assumed he did.

"Hi," he said and gave a sliver of a smile to me.

I put out my hand and he firmly shook it. "Hi, I like your store. It's cozy."

"Yeah," he grunted, "and if it gets much warmer out it's going to be stifling. Come on to the back. We can talk there."

His office was behind the partition at the back of the store and had a fake ceiling over it that a fluorescent light hung down from, illuminating the windowless-room. I hoped he didn't spend much time in there, but when I looked around and saw the piles of bills, the calculator perched on the corner of his desk, the phone at his elbow on the other side, I guessed he did. This looked like control center. On the back wall was a nature picture of two ducks on the edge of a lake. It was nicely framed with a small stamp right below it.

"That's the Minnesota duck stamp winner from a couple of years ago. Those are a couple of buffleheads. Might be worth some money someday," he told me when he saw where I was looking.

As I sat down in a naugahyde-covered chair, he gave me another jerky smile, but when it slipped off his face, what was left was sorrow. He didn't say anything for a moment, and it felt like he had fallen in on himself, could only keep up the facade of store owner, efficient older brother for so long. His black curly hair was disheveled and his plaid wool shirt wasn't tucked in. He was obviously not thinking of himself.

I wanted to put him at his ease so I commented on his business. "I suppose you don't sell many wood stoves in the spring."

"Actually we do. People do a lot of remodeling and it's a good time for them to plunk in a wood stove."

"Someday I'd love to get a wood stove, but I'm renting now and there's no place for one." He nodded and I decided to ask him why I was here, since he wasn't forthcoming. "What did you want to see me about?"

"Well, a bunch of things. Can this be totally off the record?" He swept a hand through the air.

"Sure, I didn't even bring my notebook in."

"Thanks. Well, to start, I felt like I was kind of rude yesterday at my mom's. She's having such a hard time. Bobby's dead and then the shock of Christine having the abortion and. . . . She's suffered a lot of losses all at once."

"I understand. I must say, however, that your mother strikes me as a very strong woman."

"I guess so. Sometimes I think she is but then I don't know. . . . I hate to see her so upset. I wanted to ask you again to please go through me if you need anything else from the family. I'll try to help you get the information but if you could keep her out of it."

"If it's possible, I will try to respect your request. I can't give you a promise, because I don't know what will happen in the future."

"OK, I guess that's good enough."

"Mr. Jameson, I'd like to say. . . ."

He interrupted me, "Please call me Paul."

"Sure, Paul, I wanted to tell you how sorry I am about what happened to your brother." I stopped but went ahead. I felt like he had a right to know. "I saw the bomb go off. I was standing down at the end of the hall."

"You saw it." He stood up as if he didn't know what else to do. "How could you see it? Why were you there?" He asked the question and then a possibility dawned on him.

"I was there doing a story and was on my way to talk to the director. The hallway where Bobby was standing led to the director's office."

Paul brought his hand up to his neck and circled it. "You know I've seen it again and again in my mind. I keep imagining it. How it must have been, how Bobby must have felt." His voice jerked to a stop as if it had caught on something in his throat. He cleared it and went on, "Did you see him?"

"Yes, I did."

"How was he? I mean did he know?"

"I don't think so. He smiled at me."

"Shit, that's just like him." Paul sat back down on his rolling chair and pushed away from the desk. He crossed his arms over his chest and looked down. "Stupid kid always had a smile on his face. That's why he was so good on the floor. He could sell people stoves because he was so friendly, not because he knew anything about stoves." I could hear in his voice how angry he was and I remembered feeling that anger myself. When my mom died, I wanted to yell at her for not taking care of herself. If only we'd get a chance to yell at the dead, but we didn't and often turned the anger on ourselves.

"Paul, how close were you to Bobby?"

"In some ways I was more like a father than a brother. Fifteen years older than him. After our dad died, I stepped in and tried to help Bobby out."

"He worked here for you?"

"Yeah, not real regular. When he needed money, when I needed help. He could do just about anything. Work up front in sales and help out in the warehouse. He liked working here, but he just never had a lot of drive. He'd come in late, he'd call in sick. I let him get away with that stuff. I probably shouldn't of, but he was just a kid."

"Did he talk to you much about his relationship with Christine?"

"Yeah, he'd come to me for advice although I told him I wasn't the right person. I don't have a great track record with women myself."

If Paul was going to tell me anytime it would be now, so I asked him, "Did he tell you about the abortion?"

Paul stopped and thought and that gave him away. If he hadn't known about the abortion he wouldn't have had to think about his answer, it would have been a simple no. But he had known and now he was trying to decide whether to tell me or not. He drew his breath in and said, "Yeah, he told me."

"How did he feel about it?"

"He was afraid it was going to ruin his relationship with Christine. See to him the baby was something they had done together."

"So he didn't want Christine to have the abortion?"

"I don't think he had it all worked out. He didn't know what he wanted. He was a kid. But he loved Christine and he didn't want to lose her."

* * *

On my way home I noticed the day. It was a soft spring day, not much sunshine, no rain, but definitely warmer than it had been last week. Full of promise was how it felt. I decided to swing by Tom Chasen's ex-wife's flower shop and buy myself a bouquet. Maybe she'd be there, maybe I'd get some info, but either way I'd leave with some spring flowers.

The shop was in an old building that had been newly renovated on the West Bank area near the University of Minnesota. Quite close to where I lived. There were Vietnamese and Korean restaurants, a clothing store called Global Village, and a clustering of bars where blues or reggae was played most nights. As multicultural an area as the Twin Cities got.

The storefront was all glass with a painted sign that read "Flowery Sentiments." Pots of tulips, jonquils, daffodils, and crocuses lined the ledge inside. A large vase of pussy willows arced next to the cash register and counter. From the ceiling hung baskets of ivy and spider plants.

A woman was arranging a floral piece on a table behind the counter. Wearing a yellow and blue gingham dress and blue clogs, she looked like a school girl with her hair up in braids pinned across the top of her head. Her hair was burnished gold and she had eyes as dark blue as hyacinth.

"What a wonderful shop," I said.

"Thank you." She smiled and nestled some baby's breath in among soft yellow roses.

I dug for the ex-wife's name, then asked, "Is Sheila here today?"

"Yes, that's me." She turned full around and walked up to the counter. "What can I do for you?"

She was not what I had expected. She was younger and sweeter-looking than I thought she'd be. She even wore a soft pink lipstick.

"I'd like to get some flowers."

"Great, did someone recommend me?"

"Well, I heard about you through a friend." If I wanted to get anything out of her, I couldn't start this way. "Actually though not about your flower shop. I mean he told me you had a flower shop, but.... See, I'm a newspaper reporter."

Her eyes laughed and she leaned on the counter. "It's about Tom, huh? What do you want to know?"

"Let me explain. I'm doing an article on the abortion issue—pro and con. Trying to really look at how a variety of people feel about it. The complexity of the issue, rather than only the extremes. But in the course of it, I've talked to Tom Chasen and I was trying to understand where he came from. When I was doing research I was surprised to find that he seemed to have much more liberal views in the past."

"Yeah, he left me when he left those views." She said it easily, almost casually.

"He left you?" I had assumed it had been the opposite.

"Yeah, he sure did. I'm glad now, because otherwise I might never have figured out a few things. I probably wouldn't own this shop. But it was hard at the time. We had been through a lot together. Really grew up together —college and all. Got married, were going to have a whole slew of kids and live on a farm in the country." She pulled a few dead leaves off a jade that was next to the cash register, then said, "That was a long time ago."

"What happened to change Tom?"

"There's no simple answer to that. I think it was a

85

whole bunch of things. I didn't get pregnant. Tom couldn't find a job. We lost our land. He had such high expectations that when it didn't work out he swung the other way."

She seemed so settled in herself—a very happy woman. I wondered if she had a someone in her life.

"Have you kept in touch with Tom?"

"Not really. I know what he's up to, of course. A couple times a year somebody like you comes walking in and wants to ask a few questions. Actually I don't mind. I have nothing against Tom. In fact, I kind of understand how he feels about abortion. When you can't have a child, you start to feel mad at women that get pregnant and then get rid of their chance." She got an odd look on her face, her eyes grew wider. "I'm in that process now, trying to get pregnant. In vitro. My partner Doris' brother is helping us."

"Oh, good luck." I had heard of lesbians doing that, finding a man, often a relation of their lover, who would help them out. She seemed like she would make a good mother. "Would you help me pick out some flowers?"

"Sure, what did you have in mind? Let's go look at the cut flowers in the case." She came around the side of the counter and led me to a huge refrigerated glass case with large vases full of roses, fern fronds, daffodils. In the corner I saw what I wanted—branches of leaves shaped like hearts and clusters of purple bells.

"Oh, you have lilacs. Aren't they early?"

"Yes, these are from the South. They've been flown up. I just got them yesterday so they should last the rest of the week."

I picked out enough branches for a medium-sized bouquet and she wrapped them up in thin mauve paper. When I handed her the money, she dropped it and I noticed her hand was shaking a little.

"Thank you for the flowers and for answering my questions," I told her as she gave me the bouquet and my change.

"No problem. I don't mind talking about Tom. I even have some good memories. He could be quite obsessive when he got on to something. At the time, it was one of the things that attracted me to him."

11

EVEN THOUGH it was the middle of April, the day dropped back into end-of-winter gloom. I could tell it was cold by looking out the window of my kitchen. The sky was cast-iron gray, low with scudding clouds, and the wind was rattling the barely budding tree branches around. I finished my cup of coffee and then picked up Fabiola and wrapped her around my neck. She and I went and peered out the window to look at the thermometer nailed to the house—thirty-five degrees.

This was Minnesota for you. We could have ninety-degree weather in April and we could just as easily have more snow. So we all talked about the weather like farmers, noting every nuance of degree and cloud cover. Some newcomers to the state, B.T. for instance, took it as a sign of boredom, but I had explained to him that it was much more than that. It was people trying to control the uncontrollable. Since Minnesotans couldn't talk about their feelings, another system out of control, they talked about the weather.

"Good day for a funeral," I muttered. I went to my closet and dressed with some care. Black skirt, burgundy shirt, silver pin at my throat, and over it all a black leather coat I had picked up in mint condition at a thrift shop. Going for the nostalgic look, I pulled my auburn hair back into a loose French roll.

The last funeral I had attended was my mother's and I wasn't looking forward to this one. I didn't like them. I knew they were a good ritual, a way to make the death of someone close to you more real, but I hadn't known Bobby when he was alive. Not for long, anyway. All I knew about him was his death.

* * *

The Catholic church was small, so I guessed it wasn't a cathedral. I wasn't up on the hierarchy of the Catholic buildings—at what size a structure became a cathedral or a basilica. The inside of the church was ornate and rich with dark woods that blossomed open above us in the arch of the nave. I managed to sit fairly close to the front and through most of the short service stared at Jesus in the stations of the cross around us. There was such sorrow and compassion in his face, except in the one above me, where he was carrying the cross and knows he still has a long way to go, he looked just plain dog-tired.

The church service was short and simple—closed casket, no hymns. I guessed it was the Catholic way. It seemed brusque to me and I missed the hymns of my Protestant background—"Let Me Lie with Jesus" and "Abide with Me." Singing hymns was the only time people ever sang together where I grew up in small-town Minnesota.

The Jameson family was up front in the first pew and I had a good view of them from where I was sitting. They were a handsome family. The women were all dark—one had her hair pulled back in a French braid, the next a soft page boy, and the youngest had a short cut with wispy bangs. Paul was sitting next to his mother and I watched him lean over and say something to her. She turned to him and smiled a gentle, sad smile.

Christine was sitting behind the family all by herself

and she looked tired and thin. She had lost so much in the last few days. Her eyes were dark-rimmed and her thick hair was pulled carelessly back in a loose ponytail.

As I was leaving, I wasn't surprised to see Tennison at the back of the church. Police often went to funerals; they said it was to see who else went, but often it was because they were involved—like me—and they knew the story too well not to be around for the ending.

I waited at the bottom of the steps for Tennison to come out. He looked tall and stately in his dark wool coat. "Hi," I said, "Thought I might see you here."

"Yeah, part of the job."

"What's going on these days?"

"Forensics has officially confirmed that it was a pipe bomb so you can write that up if you want."

"What's your feeling about who did it?"

"You know, Malloy, I don't have a feeling on this one. Everything points to the kid and I don't really know where else to look. I've questioned everyone at the clinic and no one saw anything unusual."

"But maybe they were used to seeing something unusual and didn't notice it anymore."

"What do you mean?"

"Those women outside parading around every morning. That's not a usual situation. They had the opportunity. Obviously they didn't walk through the clinic, but isn't there an outside access to that hallway?"

"Yes, but to come in that way someone'd have to be pretty good at locks. We didn't see any tampering, so it wasn't forced."

"Have you talked to Tom Chasen's wife, Sandy? I think she was there that day. And she certainly has the connections in the pro-life movement."

"Maybe I will have a chat with her. Thanks."

"You are looking into the fact that this bombing could

90

be motivated by the abortion issue and not just assuming it was Bobby Jameson who did it?"

"Yes and no. And besides, it's not up to me. I'm only helping the guys from homicide. Jarski's on this one. I'm sure he's aware of that, but it's a little hard to put much into that when Bobby Jameson was holding the bomb when it went off."

"I suppose, well, keep me posted."

As he walked away, I stood outside the church to the side of the sweeping steps. It wasn't raining but it was threatening to, the sky gray as an old aluminum pot cover.

I looked across the street and saw a woman wearing a scarf pulled over her forehead so it looked like a nun's wimple. Many woman still wore their heads covered in the Catholic church, a tradition they had grown up with and which I was sure was hard to discard. The woman was walking away, but turned and looked back and in that backward glance I caught sight of big glasses and little eyes that resembled Sandy Chasen's. I thought of running after her, but I had been hoping to talk to the family and to Christine and decided to shrug it off. If Sandy Chasen was at the funeral, what did it prove? What would I say to her? So I tucked it away in my information bin.

Christine came walking down the steps and nearly bumped into me. "Hey, Christine," I said, "how're you doing through all this?" She looked at me blankly and tottered slightly. I grabbed her shoulders in what might have passed for an embrace and held her steady. Up close I could see that her eyes were brimming with unshed tears.

"I don't know," she said. "I can't believe it can get any badder."

"Here," I handed her a handkerchief. I had stuffed my pockets with them, because I was sure I would need them. However, I had showed more restraint than usual. Jesus had distracted me.

"Thanks," she blew her nose, then wiped her eyes. "I just don't want to cry anymore. I feel like I'm empty of water. I want this to be all over. Are you going to the cemetery?"

"I wasn't sure."

"Oh. I just thought if you were going, we could go together."

"Do you need a ride?"

"Yeah."

"Let's go. My car's over there."

When we got to the car, I opened the door for her on the passenger side. She needed a little coddling and I wasn't sure how much more of this ceremony she was up to.

After starting the car, I managed to inch into the back of the funeral cortège and up ahead I could see the Jamesons piling into two limosines with white flags attached to the front bumpers. Mrs. Jameson stopped for a moment as Paul was helping her in and looked around. Then she said something to Paul and he shook his head. I wondered if they were looking for Christine and hoped they were. Christine was digging through her purse and didn't notice. She pulled out a lock of hair tied with a red ribbon and put it in the pocket of her coat.

"How's it going with the family?" I asked as the whole line of cars started moving.

"Not too bad. His mom has a hard time looking at me, but she's not mean. Bridget and Maddy are nice to me, because they know me, they live around here. But Kathleen hasn't really seen that much of me. I bet it'd be different if we'd been married. I'd be riding up in the limo."

"You're probably right. And Paul?"

"He's so broke up about Bobby I don't even know what to say to him. He and I used to get along fine. Not like we talked much, but we were friendly."

We rode for a bit in silence. It was odd to ride in the cortège. Driving slowly, car after car with their front headlights on, the continuous line of vehicles moved foward, running all the red lights. When I was a kid, I thought it was rather glamorous when all the rest of the traffic would stop, but now I just thought it made the driving easier.

At the cemetery, we parked and then followed everyone across the damp grass. Slightly superstitious, I avoided stepping on the flat bronze and marble markers. When we got to the top of the knoll where the open grave was, I stared down at a marker by my feet that a married couple must have bought together. Their names were carved at the top, Edwin and Myrna Thorsen, birth dates engraved below, 1910 for Edwin and 1912 for Myrna with only the death date filled in for Edwin. He had died in 1983 and Myrna was still waiting to go. There were many things I could not imagine about married life, having never been married, but there was no way I could see myself going to buy a plot with my husband.

Bobby's grave was at the top of the hill in Lakeside Cemetery and it afforded a pleasant view. The cemetery was small, made up of several rolling hills with a perfectly kept lawn and the occasional huge, gaudy mausoleum. New suburban houses skirted it and some kids on bikes were riding through the quiet lanes of the cemetery.

The dark burgundy casket was placed on a lift that went down into the hole. Mrs. Jameson walked forward and placed a dozen red roses on top of the casket and her face crumpled as she turned away. Paul stood next to her and supported her with one arm under her elbow and the other arm around her shoulders. Her sobs sounded hollow and deep in the heavy, still air of the day. Christine covered her face and I let the tears trickle down my face with an acceptance that they had finally come.

The priest stood at the head of the grave, his head bowed, his robes billowing out in the wind. We were all silent waiting for him to begin. I wiped my face. He held a small missal and started to read from it. I couldn't hear his words very well as the wind caught them and carried them off. Besides I could feel myself fall into "preacher drift" as his sing-song voice droned on. When I was a child I would float away and go off into my own world as soon as the pastor started giving the sermon.

Then everyone started reciting the Lord's Prayer and I joined in, reminding myself to stop before the Lutheran ending. The Catholics didn't add: "For thine is the kingdom and the power and the glory. Forever and ever. Amen." It sounded abrupt the way they ended it, but I stopped in time.

Christine wasn't saying anything. She wasn't praying, but her head was bent and she seemed to be folding in on herself. I wondered if she was getting cramps from standing. She didn't look like she was taking care of herself. I felt angry at the Jameson's for not taking her in. How could they blame her for what happened?

Then, just as suddenly as the service began, the graveside prayers were over. People were hugging each other and crying. The casket stayed perched up on its lift. As I recalled, they didn't lower it into the ground anymore while people were around. Too graphic.

"Can we get out of here? I don't want to stay any longer." Christine's voice was muffled through a kleenex.

"Of course."

"Wait a minute." Christine walked over to the casket and put her hand on the side of it. Her face cleared for a moment as she stared at the burnished covering. Stepping back she reached into her pocket and pulled out the lock of hair. No one was watching her except me, but she wasn't conscious of what was going on around her. The family and friends were talking and gathering together around the gravesite again. She bent over and tossed the lock of hair into the grave and turned away.

Hunching her shoulders, Christine said, "OK, I said good-bye. Let's go."

When we turned to walk away, I again saw Paul stare at Christine, but it wasn't a friendly look. I put a hand under her arm and kept her walking toward my car.

"I feel like Bobby is still around," Christine said.

I looked back at the casket, feeling like someone was following us.

"I don't mean literally," Christine went on, with the faintest chuckle. "And I know he won't stay long. But I feel him. I can't explain it better than that."

"Is it a good feeling?"

"Kind of. It's not scary. But it's a little lonely, like he's afraid to really let go of this world."

We drove for awhile in silence. I was turning on to Summit when I heard Christine make a gasp. When I looked over she was shaking all over and had her hands clenched in front of her face.

"Are you all right?"

She was crying so hard she couldn't speak.

"Christine?" I said again. Then I pulled the car over and waited a moment for her to calm down.

"I just can't stand it," she managed to spit out. The sobs sounded like wretching, they came from so deep within her. "I miss him so much. At night, I crawl in bed and it's cold and he's not there."

"I know." I thought about the missing, how it would come on when you least expected it, in the middle of a sentence or a car ride, or a sunny morning. "When my mom died I missed her so much. I used to talk to her everyday. I'd give her a call in the morning. After she died, I'd reach for the phone and then I'd remember that she wasn't there anymore. It was awful."

"I'd have the baby if he'd just come back." Her hair was falling out of her ponytail and hanging down in front of her face.

"Don't mix the two up in your mind. It wasn't your fault, Christine."

"Everything is fucked up. I lost my waitressing job. I didn't get in to work a couple times in the last few days and when I called to find out what my schedule was next week the manager said I wasn't on the schedule. He said he read about me in the paper." She wiped at her eyes and smeared hair and tears across her face. "I don't have any money. I can't pay the rent on the apartment and Bobby's not here to help. I don't know what I'm going to do."

"I know it feels impossible right now, but things will work out. Take the weekend to rest. Sleep and eat well. The first of the month is two weeks away. You'll get it together by then." I hated how cheerful I was trying to be, but I didn't know what else to say.

"Well, the worst is I don't even care. I don't care about anything. I give up. I can't do it alone. Bobby and I were going to make it together. He was going to help me go to college and everything. Now it's all over." I could hear her working herself up again.

I reached over and patted her on the back. It worked for babies. "Calm down. It will fade a little, slowly."

"Oh, god. I hurt so bad."

"Take a deep breath."

Christine took a couple quick, shallow breaths.

"No, slow down. Christine, hold them for a moment or two. Nice and easy."

She followed my instructions and then wiped her face and pulled her hair back, rebinding it with a ponytailer. She turned and looked at me and said, "Shit, I'm sorry about this. I just don't know what I'm going to do with myself."

"Have you been seeing some friends?"

"Yeah, a little. But they're freaked out. They don't know what to say to me. I think I kinda scare them."

"You might. No one ever knows what to say. When there really isn't anything you can say." I pulled back out into traffic. "Well, you seem very competent to me and even though this is hard and painful I'm betting on you."

"Thanks."

When I dropped her off at her apartment, she asked me if I'd like to come in for coffee. I told her I couldn't because I had a meeting to attend at the paper. "Listen, call if you need something. It doesn't have to be a big deal. You've got my number." I felt sorry for her and it seemed the least I could do. A few minutes on the phone. What could it hurt?

12

I WAS QUITE LATE for the editoral meeting and so I stood in the doorway, wondering if I should even bother to sit down. But when Glynda saw me, she waved me in. The meeting room was long and skinny with three windows that faced south so you could see Prospect Park and the witch's tower, which was actually an old water tower. A formica fake wood table stood in the middle of the room and chairs were strewn around it.

B.T. winked at me, Glynda wrapped her shawl tighter around her shoulders, and Bob Scale, the reporter from the crime beat, ignored me. I knew Bob was a little put out because I was following the clinic-bomb story. I squeezed into a chair next to B.T., who always sat near the door so he could slip out if the opportunity to do so presented itself. The meetings were boring, but necessary. They kept the newspaper going. We had to stay in touch with one another.

After they finished going over a new bit of policy, Glynda asked me to report in. I kept it brief because the people who needed to know, knew what I was doing, and everyone else wanted to leave. When the meeting broke up I stayed to talk to Bob. He was tall and lanky and wore glasses that he pulled on and off his nose. His focus range must have been about arm's length, because when he was talking to people he was always fiddling with his glasses—trying to see which way he could see them better. He had taken over the crime beat when I was moved up to features about two and a half years ago. He had lasted a long time on it. Most writers used it as a stepping stone, but Bob acted as though he had found his niche.

"I could use some help," I started out. "I've been off the beat long enough not to know everyone as well as I used to. What do you think of Jarski, he's the homicide detective on the clinic case. He's a new guy since I left, a transfer I think."

Bob took his glasses and stared at me, but I knew he was actually thinking. I didn't blame him for being a little pissed at me. It was a good story and they don't come by that often. But it only made sense to let me stay on it. Sliding his glasses back on, he moved in closer to me and said, "Ever see him?"

"Yeah, sure. He's short and slight. Wears a hat all the time. I think he's balding. Gray face, almost a leather face. Smokes."

"Yeah, you got it."

"How does he handle cases? Is he thorough?" I wanted to accomplish two things by talking to Bob. I hoped to smooth over any hard feelings between us and I wanted to know if there was a good way to approach Jarski.

"I'd say. But he does 'em his way. Sometimes round about."

"Have you talked to him about the Jameson story?"

"That the kid's name?"

I nodded. Bob knew that was the kid's name. He was just trying to show me how unimportant it was.

"Yeah, he's sticking with the kid. But I think he's been checking around."

"Any idea where?"

He picked up his papers from the table and straightened up. "That's it, Malloy. It's your piece—do your own legwork."

* * *

When I got home that night, it felt like the end of the very long week it had been. I did all the dishes that had been gathering in the sink since last Sunday. Then I refilled the sink and gave Fabiola a bath, which she hated. I tried to bathe her once every couple weeks because ferrets have a musky scent that can get strong and rank if not controlled. Because Fabiola was a female, the smell was milder, resembling clover honey. After her bath, I gave her a pile of towels to roll in and that kept her happy for a while, tunneling through them.

I called my dad to confirm I was coming down tomorrow. "You need anything?"

"Nope."

"You want to go out to eat?" I asked.

"Whatever you'd like."

Often we would go out to one of the couple restaurants in town. But just as often I'd bring down the makings of one of his favorite meals. He was into comfort food: tuna hot dish, blueberry muffins, vanilla pudding, even a mild chili on a cool night. I had loved these dishes as a child, so I didn't mind indulging my father by making them. There were so few ways that I could make him happy. We'd both sit around the empty house after a meal and miss my mother. She had moved through the house with speed and grace, filling it with people and talk. My father was a lonesome man without her.

After I got off the phone with my father, I looked at the clock. Eight-thirty. Too early to go to bed, but I didn't have the energy to start anything, so I took myself to a movie. A romantic movie that was sweet and dumb and that B.T. said he wouldn't go see in a million years. I liked sitting in the dark with the box of popcorn and watching a silly movie all by myself. I didn't have to explain to anyone why I wanted to go see it or why I had enjoyed it.

I got home at midnight and sat in the living room with the light on in the kitchen, but no light shining in the room I was in. I liked being in a big, empty, quiet room. I remembered my mom used to stay up late after she'd put us kids to bed. I'd come down to get something and she'd be stretched out on the couch, reading a mystery, or doing the crossword, or simply relaxing. I'd ask her what she was doing and she'd have me listen to the quiet. "I never get to hear that during the day," she'd explain. I knew there was no way around it, as I grew older I would be more and more like her.

After putting clean sheets on the bed, I climbed into it and fell into sleep, deep and comforting. I hadn't set the alarm on purpose and was planning on sleeping until I woke up.

When the phone rang, I lurched upright in bed and stared out the window. There wasn't a streak of color in the sky. What the hell time was it? I looked at my clock and tried to read the hands. It was either two-thirty or ten after six. Neither time was appealing to me and I groaned when I saw the little hand was pointing at the two.

I grabbed the phone and said, "Hello."

"You said I could call." The female voice on the other end sounded young and scared. High with tension.

"Christine?"

"Yeah, could you come over?"

"What? Now?"

"Please, there's something here and I don't know what to do with it. Maybe it should be buried."

"Christine, what are you talking about?"

"I don't want to describe it. Please come over. I brought it in the house."

"I'll be right there. Don't do anything. Stay there. I'll be there in fifteen minutes."

Undies, jeans, T-shirt, sweatshirt, socks, boots, jacket, hat, purse, and I was out the door. As I drove I tried not to think of what Christine wouldn't talk about, something that might need to be buried. I hoped my imagination went much further than the reality.

* * *

When I got to Christine's, she wouldn't open the door until I assured her several times it was me. Then she stood before me in a big T-shirt with Iggy Pop's face smiling at me. On her feet were fuzzy blue slippers. She wasn't crying but her eyes were opened wide and she looked like she was in shock.

"What's going on?" I asked as I walked past her into the kitchen area. I was afraid of what I was going to see, but all that was on the table was a blanket.

"Somebody brought this to my door, rang the bell and left." She motioned to the bundle the blanket made.

"When?"

"About a half hour ago." She held her hands out like she was carrying something. "I didn't know what else to do."

"What is it?"

"Look." She turned away, while I walked up to it.

The blanket on closer examination was a cotton blanket, trimmed with pink, for a baby's layette. I unwrapped one corner and caught a glimpse of blood and flowers. Unfolding the opposite corner, I gasped.

There was a shriveled, tiny body about half a foot long, curled up inside the blanket, completely covered with drying blood. I made out a pair of eyes closed. On top of it, crushed into the blood was a small bouquet of flowers, baby's breath, tiny pink roses. A pacifier was tied

Jarski looked back at us. "I called the medical examiner. I guess we've got to treat this thing like a body." He got up and let in Dr. Judy Schroner. A small woman with a helmet of straight black hair, she looked very pulled together for three in the morning.

I had met her several times when I was writing the crime section and found her engrossing to talk to. She was very well thought of by all the police and was known to track down oddities that other medical examiners might not feel compelled to follow up on. They talked for a second or two and then Jarski brought her over to the blanket.

Before she touched anything, Dr. Shroner pulled plastic gloves out of a large black leather bag and inched them onto her fingers. Then she gingerly lifted the edges of the blanket up, one at a time until the inside was revealed. She bent down and stared at the small figure.

At first I thought she was sniffing at it, but then realized she was looking very closely at its face. She gave a short, "huh," then lifted off the flowers and put them on the blanket next to the body. After poking at it with her finger, she turned it over, looked at something, then nodded.

She turned to Jarski and said with a little triumph in her voice, "Just as I suspected. This thing isn't human, it has a tail."

13

CHRISTINE AND I hit the road by noon after a few more hours of sleep. By one we were driving along Highway 14, headed east, just passing through Owatonna and only twenty more miles to Waseca. The sun peeked through the clouds and stayed out longer each time. The dark fields around us had water pooled on their muddy surfaces, the frost still rising out of the ground.

This rolling farmland was my psychic landscape. I had traveled out to Colorado once, looking forward to being in mountains for the first time. But when we drove up into them, I started to feel uncomfortable and the higher we went—the road getting windy and steep, the pines trees pushing around us, the tips of peaks looming above—the more I panicked and felt trapped. The slight roll of undulating farm country was all the change in altitude I could appreciate. I wanted to see the horizon around me, with a few trees and the occasional farmhouse. A cow or two was nice.

Christine had fallen asleep soon after we turned on to 35W and I envied her. It had been a long night. We didn't get back to my place until seven. I had called my dad right away and asked him if he could use a housekeeper.

He said, "No way."

I expected this. My father always said no to any sug-

108

gestion. It was his natural response. But I wasn't happy about him living all on his own down in Waseca. He was going to be seventy-six this December and he wasn't on top of things the way he used to be. After my mother died, he had suffered from depression and had gone to a doctor and been put on an antidepressant. After a few months, he took himself off of it, said it made him feel woozy. But I would feel a lot better if I knew someone saw him every day. "Wouldn't it be nice to have a housekeeper?"

"What are you talking about?" he asked.

"Someone to cook you some decent meals, do your wash, vacuum, and keep you company. All in exchange for room and board and a small fee."

I heard him thinking on the other end of the line and then he drawled, "Who'd want to do that?"

I told him. Christine was off in the bathroom, getting ready for bed, so I gave him the lowdown. I left out the part about the abortion though. My father wasn't in favor of abortions. He wasn't real strong against them, but he didn't feel they were the proper thing to do. In his mind, two people who slept together should be married and if you were married, you had kids. He accepted that I was different. He had met some of my boyfriends and I'm sure he knew I slept with them, but he didn't want to know a lot about my personal life.

"Lookit, Dad. She's almost twenty, smart, responsible, a good cook, and needs some help right now. Her boyfriend just died and she's really shook up."

"Well, she can just come down and stay for awhile."

"No, it needs to be legitimate. A real job. She needs to earn some money and get her feet under her again. It will be good for her to feel like she's doing something."

"Yeah, I see what you mean. OK. I'll figure out a few things that need doing around this place. Can she play cribbage? I'll teach her. I'll give her fifty bucks a week."

109

"A hundred."

"Highway robbery," he said, but without much force. He was struggling to keep up his image of being a curmudgeon.

My dad had sold his business, a small printing company, ten years ago and made a huge profit. He didn't do much with his money except give some to the church. He could afford to pay Christine right.

*   *   *

"What's that smell?" Christine shook her head, and wrinkled her nose.

"Did it wake you up? I hardly notice it. That is good old cow manure. Makes the corn grow."

"Yikes, it's worse than baby poop." She leaned her head against the back of the car seat and rubbed her eyes. "I was dreaming about animals. I think that skinned animal is going to haunt me for awhile."

"Christine, I'm going to let Jarski know where you are, but no one else. Jarski might want to talk to you. How does that sound?"

"All right. It's like I'm going into hiding."

"Well, you are in a way. You don't need anymore packages delivered late at night." I pulled on my sunglasses. My eyes felt gritty, like they'd been rolled in sand, but I blinked and kept driving. Not long now, I could see the next turn-off just ahead.

"What's your dad like?"

"He's quiet. Likes a routine. He reads a lot, plays cribbage."

"What's that?"

"It's a card game. One you'll probably get to know quite well."

Christine bent her head from side to side. I thought of stopping so we could both stretch our legs, but we were almost there. My favorite barn was coming up on the right—a landmark I watched for when I drove home. Its weathered sides showed a few remaining traces of red, but the cedar-shingled roof was sagging in the middle like a swayback horse. I was always afraid I'd drive by and it would be gone.

"Why does your dad want a housekeeper?" Christine asked.

"Well, he doesn't exactly. I mean, he doesn't think he needs one, but I do. He's getting up in years and every once in a while I'll call him and he'll just seem out of it to me. Now, maybe I've caught him at a bad time, maybe he woke up from a nap or something, but I wouldn't mind someone down there keeping an eye on him, keeping him company and keeping him fed. I don't think he eats too well. He's not much of a cook and I think he'd rather just grab something than fix himself a meal." I gave Christine the impression that she'd be doing me a favor to watch out for my dad and I'd told my dad that he'd be helping Christine out if he'd let her stay for awhile. But both were true.

"What did you tell him about me?"

"Just the basics. That I was doing a story when I met you. That your boyfriend just died and you needed a place to stay. I didn't tell him about the abortion. He's not in favor of them, although I don't think he's given it much thought."

"Fine. I don't want to talk about it anyway." She turned her face toward me and confided, "God, it's a relief though to feel better. I was so sick the last few days I was pregnant. They call it morning sickness, but with me it was all day long. I'd kid Bobby and ask him if he could take a turn being pregnant for awhile." She rubbed her stomach.

"What was it like, the abortion?"

"Not as bad as I thought. Like a long pelvic examination. The doctor had an accent and I remember him telling me over and over again that I was doing good. There was this sucking noise and then I could see the blood running into a pan. He told me the fetus was too little to see, but I didn't believe him. Not that I wanted to see it. I think about it a lot. It would've been a baby. Right before the abortion, I tried to tell it it was nothing personal. That at another time I would have felt different."

I could hear by the sound of her voice that she was close to tears. I pointed out the window. "Look how dark the earth is around here."

"Does your dad have a garden?"

"Usually, but he didn't put one in last year." When I was growing up, we lived out of the garden—corn, green beans and wax beans, tomatoes, radishes. My mother would eat radish sandwiches for lunch.

"Oh, I'd love to do a garden."

I thought of something I hadn't asked her about. "Paul told me that he knew about the abortion. He said Bobby had told him about it. Did you know that?"

"No, but it doesn't surprise me. He and Paul were so close. They talked about everything. Anyway, Paul had a girlfriend who had one. So I'm sure that Bobby felt comfortable talking to him about it."

"Paul had a girlfriend who had an abortion?" This surprised me. He hadn't let on at all to me. This probably did confuse the issue of his brother's death for him. He had gone through what his brother had—up to a point.

"Yeah, it was maybe four or five years ago. Before I was going out with Bobby. But he told me. We didn't keep secrets from each other much."

"What happened to the girlfriend?"

"I don't know. She was already gone when I came on the scene. Paul hasn't gone out with anyone steady since I've known him. He hangs around with women. He's good-looking so I don't think he has any trouble, but he just hasn't connected with one."

Paul *was* good-looking.

I could pull up snapshots of him in my mind as I was driving—in his leather jacket at his mom's, his sad eyes at the store, his stiffness at the funeral. I wondered why he hadn't hooked up with anyone and then I thought of my own record. I could connect with men all too easy, I just couldn't stay with them. Who knows what his problem was.

* * *

When we drove into Waseca, I was watching Christine. This was the town she was going to spend at least a few weeks in and she had never lived in a small town before. Waseca has only 8,219 people in it. I thought of telling Christine a little about the town but I decided she had enough to absorb. She was staring out the window of the car, and I could see she was giving in to what was happening to her.

The farmland faded quickly and then we were driving along Clear Lake, angling into town. The street was lined with old houses that were already old when I was a child. We drove by the florist, a painted rose on the sign out front, and I pointed out the attached greenhouse. I had run down the aisles of it as a child and stood on tiptoe to see the growing plants. We went by the library and I told her she should go get a card, it was within walking distance of my dad's house.

I pulled into the driveway and stopped and looked at the house I grew up in with new eyes. It was an old white farmhouse with a porch the whole length of the front. A swing was hanging in the porch, but other than that it was empty. Too cold to sit and take a gander at the neighbors.

"This is it?" she asked.

"Yup."

"This reminds me of *Anne of Green Gables*. You ever read that book? It's how I imagined it." She turned to me and said with wonder, "Do you know that I've never lived in a house. I've always lived in apartments. This place is huge."

"Dad's shut off a couple of the rooms, but when I was little my brother and I each had our own room and Mom had a sewing room."

"God, a sewing room. What a luxury." She undid her seat belt, then reached down and got her purse off the floor of the car. She opened it, then closed it, then opened it, then looked at me. "How long are you going to stay?"

"I'll stay for a few hours. We can have a late lunch together and then I've got to get back to town." I touched her on the shoulder, "Before we go in, I want to say something. You're doing me a big favor, Christine. My dad's been real lonely since my mom died. He stays at home a lot and I'm afraid he's been getting kind of reclusive. It'll be nice for me to know that he's got company for a while."

"No problem. I just hope we get along."

* * *

James Malloy, my father, stood in the doorway, holding the screen door open as Christine and I came up the steps. In his seventy-sixth year, he was still over six feet tall, but had thinned down so his cheekbones stuck out and his eyes looked sunken in. His eyes were watery blue and sharp; glasses framed them and enlarged them slightly. As he came forward to greet us, I noticed his bum leg was bothering him as he was favoring it.

"Give me that bag." He reached down and took Christine's duffel from her. She had no real luggage so we had put her clothes in a variety of smaller bags, had even used a grocery bag.

"Hi, Mr. Malloy." Christine stood in front of him on the porch and held out her hand.

"Hi, kid. Let me show you your room."

Over the phone we had agreed that she should take my brother Jake's since he came home so rarely from Montana. I let Dad take her upstairs and I walked through the house. Dad had started storing all his shoes and boots in the entryway and kept an old pair of slippers there to slide into when he got home. Mom would never have let him get away with that.

A week's worth of papers was stacked at the end of the dining room table, near to the kitchen, where he ate his meals. The shades were still drawn in the dining room and I opened them all, let a little sunshine in. Mom's old furniture—the oak table, the buffet, and several small tables—could stand a dusting. I had asked Dad to get someone in and do it once a month, but he wouldn't. He said he wasn't busy, he had time to clean the house, but he either didn't do it or he didn't know how to do it.

The kitchen floor was splattered with spills. When I opened the refrigerator, it looked full, but on careful examination, I found rotting apples, limp carrots, wilted lettuce. Seeing the house in this state of neglect made me sad. My mom would have been so upset that it was like this. And I felt I was seeing the real state of my father's mental health. He just plowed through the days, not taking care of himself.

I dug out some eggs and checked the expiration date. Still good enough for an omelette. There were potatoes and cheese and onions. I decided to fry up a decent breakfast, even if it was two-thirty in the afternoon.

* * *

115

After our late lunch, Christine went up to her room to lie down and I read the Sunday paper with my father. We had always been a family that read together. We'd gather in the living room and a comfortable silence would fill it. Once in a while someone would read something to the others, but usually we'd be engrossed in our own books.

"I saw your piece on that kid who got blown up at the clinic," my dad said, not looking up from the paper.

"Oh, yeah." I hadn't thought of that.

"This Christine the girlfriend?"

"Yeah." I waited to hear what he had to say about that.

"She's had a tough time, huh?" He folded the paper and laid it in his lap.

"Yeah."

"Seems like a good kid."

"I think so."

"Where are her folks?"

"Never knew her dad, her mom's in Florida. They're not in touch."

"I just hope she can cook. Doctor said I gotta quit eating eggs. My cholesterol, you know. But I've been living on eggs."

"Well, let Christine know that." I looked at him. The afternoon sun was coming in the window and his eyes were sagging. It was past time for his nap. "You getting out much these day?"

"The usual. Church. Play cribbage with the old fogies at the Senior Center on Tuesdays. I'm fine."

* * *

When I was just about to leave, Christine asked, "What should I do now?"

I was standing in the entryway and had finished lining up the piles of shoes against the wall. "Make a grocery list.

There's hardly any food in the house."

"OK," she said, but stared at me with slight panic in her eyes.

"Ask my dad what he wants to eat. He'll tell you. But first you might want to clean out the refrigerator and throw anything away you think might be funky."

"That's a good idea." She looked into the living room where my dad was reading the paper. "I'll start to work on that. Will he want to eat again tonight?"

"Probably. Ask him." They still didn't know what to call each other. For some reason, Dad had fastened on "kid," and Christine was simply avoiding the issue by calling him nothing. I figured they'd work it out.

She turned and walked up to him. He didn't lower the paper. She reached out a hand and tapped it. Crumpling it, he started at the sound.

"Do you want to eat again?" she asked.

"What did you have in mind?"

Just like my father to ask her a question, instead of answering hers. Actually reminded me of myself.

Christine stood thinking for a moment and then said, "How about grilled cheese sandwiches?"

"Grilled cheese sandwiches. That sounds good." I saw a hint of a smile cross his lips before he lifted the paper up again. They'd do fine.

* * *

When I got home all I wanted to do was fall into bed, but I needed to check in with Jarski and B.T.—Jarski to find out the news on the animal delivered to Christine and B.T. for a sanity check. And Paul Jameson had left a message on my machine. I wondered what he wanted.

Jarski told me someone had skinned the animal, that it was at least a week dead, and it had been identified as a red squirrel from this region. "But there were no prints on anything, not the pacifer or anything."

"Do you think it's connected to the bomb?"

"Sure, I do, but maybe not directly. In other words, if you're asking me did the person who set the bomb also give Christine the squirrel, I doubt it. Some weirdo could have read about it in the paper, picked her name up from there and decided to deliver her a fake baby. I don't know."

B.T.'s machine picked up after two rings and I heard his rapid-fire voice say, "Don't hang up. This is your chance of a lifetime. If you leave your name and particulars, the man of your dreams will call you back. So, go ahead, give it all you've got."

"Yeah, yeah, yeah, B.T. where are you? Are you watching some dumb game and can't be bothered to pick up your phone? This is Laura in dire distress."

A click came over the line and he asked, "How dire?"

I told him.

"You must be plumb tuckered."

"I am. Did I do the right thing?"

"You mean interfering with this poor girl's life, dragging her down to your dad's and indenturing her for the rest of her days. Sounds all right to me."

"I got too involved, didn't I?"

"Of course you did. That's all right, Laur. That's what we love about you."

"What are you doing tonight?" I was collapsing from lack of sleep, but I also had that jittery charged feeling from hours of driving and strong emotion. A bit of talk and a nightcap might be good for me.

"I got a date."

"You don't. B.T., did you ask out Josy?"

"Yup." B.T. had been threatening to ask out this cute young thing that worked in the library at the newspaper. She was twenty-one, enthusiastic, always smiling and giggling. I thought she was too young and too sweet for him, but what did I know?

"Well, take it slow."

"Listen, I hardly know what first base looks like." We signed off.

Finally Paul. It took three calls to track him down. First I tried the store, it was closed. Second, I tried his home. Nothing. Finally I tried his mother's. She answered the phone with a soft hello.

"Mrs. Jameson," I was back on formal terms with her. "This is Laura Malloy. Paul called me and I wondered if he was there."

"Yes, he's been worried about Christine. He'd like to talk to you. You were with her at the funeral, weren't you?"

I wanted to say "and you weren't," but I held my tongue. "Yes, I thought she needed a little support."

Meg Jameson only said yes, but I thought it might have hit home. "Let me get Paul," she said and left the phone. In a few moments, I heard Paul's voice, low and gravelly, "Yeah?"

"Hi, Paul, this is Laura Malloy. You called?"

"Yes. I tried to call Christine a couple times. She's not answering her phone. I thought you might know where she is."

"Why?"

"Well, she didn't come over here yesterday, and now she's gone. I saw you with her, didn't you drive her home or something? Did she tell you what she was going to do?"

"Why do you want to talk to her?" I didn't know what I should tell him.

"You do know where she is? I'd like to talk to her about things."

"I think she's gone out of town for awhile. This all has been too much for her."

119

"Yeah, well, I've just been worried about her." Paul paused, took a breath, then suggested, "Do you feel like meeting me for a drink?"

I did want a drink and I did feel like I had more to learn from Paul Jameson. "Where?"

"You know the Turf Club?"

"On University?"

"Yeah, that's the one. How about meeting me there in an hour?"

I looked down at my jeans and sweatshirt. My hair was pulled back in a haphazard ponytail. I was sweaty from driving three hours and tired as hell. "Sounds good."

14

THE TURF CLUB was on University Avenue, only a half a block from one of the best used bookstores in the Twin Cities and about a mile from my office. But I had never been there before. The facade of it was aging, the neon lettering of *The Turf Club* partially unlit. It shared a parking lot with a bank and I wondered how many customers cashed checks and then walked over and spent part of them.

When I walked into the Club, I was surprised by how dark it was. The place looked like a real joint to me. A single light dangled over the pool table, the stage was dimly lit, and hanging from the ceiling were some old art deco colored light fixtures, which gave off a vague glow. An old mahogany bar stretched all along the back of the room and at the front was a small dance floor with a country-western band playing.

I didn't see Paul so I slowly walked to the bar. I was still surprised I had agreed to come down here to meet him. I didn't really trust him. One thing I wanted to make clear to him was that this was not a date or anything remotely resembling one. There isn't any big rule about not going out with someone you are interviewing for the paper, but it's not a good idea. Mixing business and pleasure is never a good idea, but sometimes, in my life, it felt like they got put together in a blender.

I walked up and leaned on the end of the bar so I could get the lay of the place. Looking around the room at the clientele, I didn't see anyone under fifty, except the members of the band: Lynette White and the Rednecks. Lynette was not Dolly Parton but she was hoping. Her mass of blonde curls sat slightly crooked on her head, and she had a voice that had sung through too many boozy nights, but it had heart. She was singing "Walking After Midnight" and the words hit home, reminding me of my rambling days out late at night in bars, looking for love, which I hoped were over. And yet here I was tonight, trying to tell myself it was for work, research for a story.

As I searched the room again, I didn't sight Paul, but then I was, as usual, a little early. A habit of mine. I had found that a sure way to make someone you're interviewing angry, when they already think they're giving you too much of their time, is to be late. So I just wasn't. Paul, on the other hand, had to extricate himself from his family. A little harder than plunking Fabiola in her closet.

The bartender asked me what I'd have and I told him I'd take a tap beer—Leinenkugel's. He said they didn't serve tap beer while the band was playing. I asked him if they had Leinie's in a bottle. He said no, no bottles, only cans. I was really feeling like a snot by this time, but I hate the flavor of beer in a can, the metal makes the beer taste flatter and more bitter.

"I'll have a shot of tequila with a beer back," I said. That way I'd get a tap beer, and I liked tequila. I liked knowing it came from a wild desert plant growing south of the border. A bit of sunshine on a sodden spring day never hurt anybody.

Feeling a hand on my shoulder, I turned and saw Paul. His leather jacket was unzipped and looked like he had thrown it on. He was squinting his eyes, from fatigue I assumed.

"Hi," I said.

"Yeah, hi, hope you haven't been waiting long. It wasn't that easy to get away, but...." He paused for a second, looking me full in the face. "I'm awful glad I did."

"This is a weird place." I looked away and gestured at the bar.

"Yeah, haven't you ever been here before?"

"No, I've driven by and noticed it, but never been inside. How did you happen to discover it?"

The bartender put down my shot of tequila and glass of beer. Paul pulled out a twenty and set it down on the bar in front of my drink and ordered a Johnny Walker Red on the rocks.

"I can get this," I said, digging in my purse.

When I tried to put down the money, he pushed my hand away, "You get the next one. All right?"

"Sure."

I took a sip of tequila and couldn't think of a thing to say to him. I wanted to find some things out—like about his girlfriend's abortion, his attitude toward Christine, but I couldn't figure how to slip them into conversation. And I was tired. My usual ability to talk about nothing vanished when fatigue set in. In the mirror behind the bar I could see Paul's face and I noticed that he had a good nose. It was the right size for his face and was aquiline, a word I had always liked.

I heard him say something and turned back toward him. "I know this place because a buddy of mine went to Hamline and we used to come over here and drink. We'd come during the day, and drink cheap beer and eat Adeline's homemade soups and play pool. That was a while ago." He looked around at the place. "I don't remember it being such a dive. I don't really go out much these days."

"Did you go to college?" Feed him questions, I thought, that's what you're good at.

"For awhile. I went in chemistry, but never got a degree. Went to the U and I'm glad I did, but then I started the store and been making a good living off that ever since. Did you go to the U?"

"Yeah, majored in journalism, but where I learned the most was working on the *Daily*."

"Oh, yeah, I used to read that." Glancing up at the blinking Budweiser beer sign over the bar, Paul spaced out on me for a moment. I recognized the blank look in his eyes. His head was tilted back and he seemed to be catching his breath. His black hair had been slicked back into the semblance of a groomed look, but the curls were creeping out. Shaking his head, he said, "OK. So do you know where Christine is?"

"Yes, but she doesn't want anyone to know."

"Why? Did something happen?"

Why did he jump to that conclusion? Could he have been trying to get hold of Christine to find out her reaction to the squirrel wrapped in a baby blanket? Could he have delivered it? "Yes, as a matter of fact. Her boyfriend was killed."

"God, I know that."

"And your family could be helping her out a little."

He bent his head down and shrugged his shoulders. "You're right. I know Mom feels bad, but she's having a hard time talking with Christine. She can't help but feel that Christine is responsible for what happened."

"Then it's probably just as well that she doesn't talk to Christine for awhile." I got defensive about Christine— couldn't they see that she was just a kid? "She's already blaming herself enough as it is."

124

"You know, I'm having trouble too." Paul looked past me and spoke slowly, as if he'd said it before. "Doesn't the guy ever have a say in this abortion stuff? It's his child too. What if he wants it?"

"Well, for one thing, it isn't a child. And for another when a couple decide to use birth control, they are making a decision together about whether they want her to get pregnant."

"People can change their minds."

"Did Bobby want the pregnancy?"

"Yeah, as a matter of fact he did. But don't tell the police that, they'll think it proves something."

Paul ordered another drink and I managed to pay for it. I was still sipping my tequila, letting the fiery fuel go down my throat real slow. I took my time drinking a shot of tequila. I rarely chugged them anymore. Tequila could sneak up on you way too fast that way.

"Let's go grab that booth," Paul pointed to a booth up close to the dance floor. As we walked toward it, he took my arm and I felt awkward, not wanting this kind of attention from him.

When we settled in, the waitress came and asked us how we were doing. I thought it was a very good question. I sure didn't have the answer. I covered my glass with my hand and told her I was doing fine. She turned to Paul so I had a chance to stare at her. Somewhere in her sixties, she was something to see. Her hair was shaped into curls that formed a helmet of fake blackness around her head and matched her painted-on eyebrows. Her glasses had rhinestones in the corners. I wondered if she had been working at the Turf Club that long and if her black waitress outfit was an original. Paul ordered another whiskey and she shuffled away to get it.

"How's everybody in your family handling getting written up in the paper?"

125

"Not bad."

"Did your mom feel all right about what I wrote about Bobby?"

"You couldn't have said enough good things about Bobby to please my mother, so don't even think about it. Bobby's on his way to sainthood right now. Right up there with my dad, who was anything but. I thought it was fine. Didn't go overboard. I mean, how can you write about someone you don't know?"

"That's what I have to do just about every day."

"Yeah, well, I thought it was fine." He said it like it ended that conversation. I didn't mind. I sat back in the booth and listened to the music. They were playing a song I didn't recognize, but it was catchy and fast and if I had had more energy I'm sure some part of my body would have been moving to it.

Paul touched my hand to get my attention. "Can you dance like that?" he asked me.

I turned and watched the people spinning around on the dance floor. I picked out one couple who were the best dancers. The woman had short dark hair and the guy was wearing a black cowboy hat and between them they had to weigh over five hundred pounds, but they were floating around the dance floor. They would move together in a simple shuffle step and then he would spin her around and it looked so easy.

"Nope, what are they doing?"

"The two-step."

"I can waltz and polka, but I've never two-stepped." I hoped he wouldn't ask me to dance. Normally I loved to get out on the floor and goof around, but tonight I was finding it difficult enough to lift the glass of liquid to my lips and back to the table.

Since it was going to be in the paper, I decided to tell him what had happened to Christine last night. I wanted to watch his face as I told him. I didn't go into great detail, didn't tell him that we thought it was a fetus for awhile, didn't tell him about the flowers or pacifier. But I think he got the picture. And as far as I could tell by the expressions on his face, it was all news to him.

"Some people out there have sick minds. Doing shit like that. I'd like to get my hands on the guy who did that."

"You think it's a guy?"

"Well, I don't know. But it takes a certain amount of guts to go walking around in the middle of the night, leaving a package at somebody's doorstep. Besides, I just can't imagine a woman doing something so weird."

"Huh, I can. Woman don't often come out and fight, but they have their tricks for getting a point across and they're often cruel about it." I thought of Sandy, wearing her amulet in hopes of getting pregnant, and wondered if she were capable of such an action.

Paul looked at me and asked, "Are you going to put this in the paper?"

"Yes," I said.

"How can you do that? Doesn't it seem like an invasion of Chris's privacy?"

"I don't think that everything that happens to us should go in the paper, but what happened to Christine last night might have bearing on the bomb incident. People need to know what's going on. It's the way we monitor the world around us."

He looked down at his glass, then shook his head. "How do you do what you do? Digging into other people's lives?"

I didn't want to defend myself. I was too tired, it was too late and I liked him too much. Nothing I did made much sense to me in the dim light of the bar so I thought back to how I had started in this business. "You know it's

127

funny. I'm where I am because I like to write. I was the editor of my high school newspaper. I liked being where things were going on, the deadlines, all that excitement. But the longer I do it, the more I'm caught up in the stories. Who people are, why they do what they do. I'm fascinated by it all. And trying to write the truth. That's a hard thing to do."

"The truth, fuck, who even knows what it is. There's so many points of view, reasons for things happening." He lifted up his glass and took a swallow. "I think the truth is a lie."

There was something I had wanted to know the answer to for a while and decided to ask him. "Do you think Bobby brought that bomb to the clinic with him?"

Paul ducked his head and at first I thought he was avoiding the question, but then I wasn't sure. He was pinching his nose at the bridge as if he had a migraine. He cleared his throat a few times, then finally said, "You told me what Bobby looked like when you saw him. I'll never forget what you said, 'He looked up at me and smiled.' Now, does that sound like someone who knows they're about to be blown up?"

"No, but he wouldn't have thought that. The bomb malfunctioned. Something set it off early."

"I don't think Bobby had any idea what was going on. He wasn't dumb, but he just didn't think things through. Who knows what happened? Whatever went on I know that Bobby would never hurt anyone. He just didn't have it in him."

"I have a feeling the police aren't seeing it that way. From the information I've gotten from them, they're starting to think that Bobby's the perpetrator."

"Goddamnit. It's convenient for them to think that, to look no further. They can wrap up the case and forget about it." Paul looked toward the band and said, "It's go-

128

ing to tear my mom up. She's had a hard enough time of things already, but now to have to live with the fact that society thinks your son did such a crime."

"Well, maybe something will turn up. They're still investigating . . . and so am I."

"Will you keep me posted on what you find out? And if there's any way I can help out, let me know."

We talked a little more. I could tell Paul was nearly as tired as I was. I was holding on to the night with my fingernails and it was slipping away. The music stopped, the dancers left the floor, and we had empty glasses in front of us.

Paul rocked his glass back and forth between his large hands. "It wasn't like this when my dad died."

I watched his hands and waited.

"I was almost glad. He was mean to me, to all us kids. He drank. I still was sorry and all, but not like this." He held a hand over the top of the glass as if to keep something from escaping. "Bobby was just a kid. I feel like a part of me is gone, like someone cut a hunk of flesh out of my stomach."

In the dark of the bar, I saw a flash and then the blood was everywhere. The noise was an echo in my mind. A smiling kid dead. I shook my head to clear it. Paul was a little drunk and deeply sad. I didn't know what to do with him. I stood up and said, "Let's get out of here."

We were quiet as Paul walked me to my car. The air was misty, it felt soft and good on my face. My trusty Dodge Dart was parked crooked between a Harley Davidson and a dumpster.

"This is it." I slapped the rear left fender.

"Nice car," he said, looking at me.

"Gets me places." I wondered what he wanted.

"Sorry I was such bad company."

"You were fine."

He reached out and touched my hair. "I like the color of your hair. It looks like mahogany. A rich color."

"Thanks," I said and decided not to tell him it was hennaed.

His hand fell to my shoulder and he didn't say anything. I pulled away, but he stopped me. "I'd like to go out again some time."

I looked straight at him and said clearly, "Listen, Paul, let's see what happens. I'm working on a story on your brother and I'm glad that you've taken the time to talk to me. But, for right now, I have work to do."

Paul tipped his head back and laughed. The laugh transformed him into someone I might want to see again. He squeezed my arm and then let go of it. He took a step away and then said, "But, see, I like you. Maybe when this is all over, I'll ask you again." He turned and walked away.

* * *

When I got home that night, the red light was blinking on my answering machine so I flipped back to the one message. I was taking off my coat when a thin female voice came on: "Laura Malloy, I need to talk to you. It's horrible what we've done. This is Sandy Chasen. Please call me. Don't let Tom know. Please don't let him know."

She stopped talking and I thought the message was over but then she added, "I need to talk to someone about the babies."

15

So I dreamed about them. Babies popped out of the ground. They sprang forth in buds, in cornfields, rows of them. Their arms were waving, their mouths open. The sound of gurgling filled the air. Then a river of red surged up, blood spilling from some of the babies and running down between the rows in rivulets. The sound changed to a roar and I yanked myself out of sleep.

After that first moment of taking in breath like it would save me, I felt the night still and empty around me, and lay with my arms folded over the covers and my head back on the pillow. I stared at what I could see of the ceiling. My curtains let in a slit of light from the street lamp and it cut across my ceiling in a way that made it appear like the door to someplace else.

It was simple. I was in over my head. I was getting crazy phone calls from the subordinate wife of the head of the anti-abortion movement in Minnesota and I was being asked out by the brother of a man I had seen blow up. There was no explaining any of it. There didn't seem any place to go but forward. I needed to contact Sandy Chasen. She obviously knew something and was ready to tell someone about it. After all, it was my job to be that someone.

I glanced over at the clock and saw it was four in the

morning. I had only gone to sleep a few hours ago and didn't want to get up. So I closed my eyes and waited for the babies to go away. While I did, I wondered if I would ever have one. Having a child seemed like one of the scariest things you could do and one of the most rewarding, but so far away from my life. On the screen that played inside my brain, the chubby legs of babies vanished from view and I fell back into slumber.

* * *

When I woke next, my room was filled with sunlight and a little critter was snuggled in next to my ear. Fabiola yawned as I sat up and then she stretched and yawned again. When I reached out to pet her, she went under the covers and burrowed down to my feet, nipping at them when I moved. Sliding a hand down slowly, I found her and pulled her out, then cradled her back in my palm, her head and tail hanging over.

"You want to go for a walk today?" I asked, but I already knew the answer. She loved to run around the house, but she didn't like to be outside—the noise and the direct sunlight bothered her because she was an albino. She skulked and looked for cover and, even though I had a leash on her, I was afraid she'd find some hole and disappear down it. It was what ferrets were meant to do.

The phone rang and I lunged for it, hanging half off the bed. "Good morning," I said pleasantly, trying to disguise the sleep tendrils clinging to my voice.

"B.T. here."

"Hey, B.T. You want to go for a walk?"

"Outside?"

"What, you've gotten so old, we have to do it in a mall?"

"How about just settling for breakfast? That's about as much exercise as I can take this morning."

"Don't tell me you've had an exhausting night with Josy?" I had trouble imagining what they found to talk about, although at work she laughed at everything he said.

"Kind of."

"Where do you want to meet?"

"Seward, OK?"

"Fine by me."

Only three blocks from my house, the Seward Cafe was right next to the Seward Co-op and had sprung from the same hippie spirit some twenty years ago. It was a small brick building with a garden in back and an outdoor patio, but on this brisk spring day, I looked for B.T. inside. The cafe had expanded but it had kept all its dilapidated charm, while spreading out to fill another room. It still had booths with seats that had hills and valleys in them, and a long bar where you stood and ordered your food.

I found B.T. slumped into the corner of the last booth, reading the *New York Times,* which he and I fondly called "the other *Times.*" He wanted to write for it someday and I wasn't so sure I did, but, like him, I loved reading it on Sunday mornings.

I had thrown on cowboy boots, sweatpants and a decent red wool sweater to walk over. After splashing water on my face and making a pass at my teeth, I felt ready for the world I would encounter at the Seward. They were not a critical bunch. B.T.'s hair was sprouting at angles I had never seen before. He was wearing a black turtleneck, which made him look like a turtle, with a faded, torn jean jacket over that and then, over it all, a maroon down vest.

"You're looking pretty sassy today," I remarked.

"What does that mean?" he growled.

"My, my, a little touchy. Have you had any coffee?"

He lifted up his half-empty cup. "I just wish I could mainline it."

133

"So do you want to tell me about your night or listen to mine?"

He slurped his coffee and nodded his head at the second part of the sentence so I launched into the day before with Christine and Paul and finally Sandy and her cryptic mention of the babies.

"When are you going to talk to Mrs. Sandy Chasen?" B.T. asked.

"I'm going to try today. I don't know, hubby's probably going to be around, but I thought I could do a stakeout of their house and see if the coast is clear."

"I could call and ask to speak to him," B.T. volunteered.

"I don't think we need to go undercover for this one, but if I don't get through to her easily, I might take you up on it."

"What do you think they're doing to the babies?"

"Lord, B.T., who knows what she's talking about. She's an odd one. Maybe she just wants to talk some more about the abortion clinic. I hope so."

"Maybe she and her husband are digging through dumpsters and finding aborted fetuses."

Suddenly huevos rancheros with their red hot sauce didn't sound as appetizing. "I did think of that. I don't know if that's possible. I thought they passed a law that you had to get rid of the remains in a respectful manner."

"Better check into it."

We both wrote out our orders—I stuck with plain eggs and a side of hash browns, but B.T. got the "whole earth combo" which had all sorts of root vegetables cooked in an egg mixture—and then settled back into the booth.

"OK, time for a recap of your night," I pressed him.

"She's smarter than she looks," he started.

"Good," I said, thinking of her tight fitting angora sweaters over short skirts and high heels.

134

"Why are you being so hard on her? After all, she likes me."

"Well, there's that for starters," I rejoined. "I just don't trust anyone who giggles that much."

"But that's because I make her laugh."

"I don't mind laughter, it's giggles that put me on edge."

"God, Laura, ease up. She has a rather high-pitched laugh, but it's better than your snort."

"I'm fussy about who goes out with you. You know that." I drank my coffee and sighed. Almost a meal unto itself the way I fixed it up—heavy cream and honey. "So what did you guys do last night?"

"She had me over for dinner."

"That's not what you do on a first date." I sat up and glared at B.T. "That's third or fourth date activity."

"It was her idea. She said she wanted to try out a new recipe for veal cacciatore. She's Italian."

Our names were called and we went to pick up our food. Looking at the mound of eggs à la earth on B.T.'s plate, I wondered how good her cooking had been. His appetite was large this morning. I decided to ease up on him. He seemed to like Josy and I sensed I shouldn't push him too much or he would turn snarly.

"Did you have a nice time?" I asked him when we sat down.

"Yeah, you could say that." He mumbled something with his mouth full and I missed it.

"What?"

"She's got a kid."

"She's got a kid?"

"Yeah." he looked at me with great sorrow etched on his face. "A five-year-old."

"No shit. Boy or girl."

"Little boy. Big eyes just like hers. His name is Tony.

135

He was staying at a friend's house, but I saw pictures of him."

"I didn't realized she'd been married."

"She hasn't. She got pregnant when she was in high school, living at home and she said there was no way she could have had an abortion. Catholic and all. So she had the kid, lived at home, and made it through college. This is her first job, she and Tony now have their own place and she's making a go of it. I like her, she's got gumption."

"Yeah, sounds like it."

"But I don't know about this kid stuff. I don't even want my own. Why would I want someone else's?"

"So you slept with her?"

"Laura, why must you jump to these conclusions?"

"Because I know you—you like her, and why else would you be worried about her kid. You slept with her."

"It was her idea."

"What? She talked you into it? Give me a break."

"No, but I was getting ready to leave. I mean, I even had my jacket on and everything and then . . ."

"OK, OK. I'm not up to details today."

"Are you jealous?"

I looked at him with what I hoped was horror. Jealous of someone else sleeping with B.T.? "No, B.T., you're my best friend in the world, but I'm glad to let others take care of your sexual needs."

"No, I meant, jealous because you're alone."

I ate a couple bites of food. I needed more energy to answer that. "Well, you might have something there. I don't want a guy to come in and take over my life and yet when I'm not seeing anyone, it's a little boring. I can only work so many hours a day."

"Well, if I may do a little Malloy analyzation here, you don't give yourself a break. You are still pulling away from Gary. You need some time. Ease up on yourself."

"I won't be critical of Josy; in fact, to be honest what you told me about her makes me like her better. But get her to wear less makeup. And don't disappear completely, just because you're seeing her."

"Sure, in fact, maybe you could meet us for a drink some night?"

"Stop."

* * *

I spent the afternoon cleaning. I decided to rearrange my books and had the thought to arrange them alphabetcially and by categories: non-fiction, fiction, poetry. I had taken all the books off the shelves, plus brought out all the piles of books that had been lurking under the couch, behind the bed, in the room I called my office. Someday I was going to write something longer than a newspaper article. Someday I was going to write a book, an important book on a big subject, so I needed to read books to see how it was done. But at the moment, I had managed to totally trash my apartment.

Looking around the living room at leaning piles of alphabetically ordered books, a small white ferret snuffling among them all, I decided it was time to drive by the Chasen household and see who was home. This task could be done late at night when I didn't feel like watching TV.

I took the slow route around Lake Calhoun to Edina. The city of Minneapolis has nine lakes within its boundaries and they are extremely accessible with walking paths and biking paths and of course, rollerblading paths. The soft late afternoon sun had drawn people out of their houses and they were moving in formation, circling the lakes. I saw an older couple in their middle fifties, holding hands at the crosswalk, and felt a lump in my throat for the quiet contentment that shone on their faces. I wasn't sure if

I was feeling sorry for myself or for my father and what he had lost. The light changed and I drove around the northern tip of the lake and then continued on Excelsior Boulevard.

When I reached the Chasen house a few minutes later, dusk was settling over the neighborhood. I parked my car across the street and down a house. I wouldn't be able to stay indefinitely. In a neighborhood like this, someone would call the police to report an unknown car with an unknown person sitting in it for too long. I slumped down in the seat and listened to a country western radio station. They played "Runaway Train" by Roseanne Cash and it sent my mind drifting back to last night and what might have happened.

I couldn't tell what was going on at the Chasens'. A silver gray Saab was parked in the driveway and as I recalled that was Tom's car, but the garage door was closed and so I didn't know whether Sandy's car was in there or not. Looking over their front lawn, I saw green spears peeking up along the turned-up soil at the front of the house. They looked like the beginnings of a crocus patch and I remembered Sandy puttering around in that front garden.

It really didn't make much sense to be here on a Sunday. Tom would be gone to work on Monday and I'd have a much better chance getting to Sandy then, but it was hard to wait. Even driving over here made me feel like I was doing something. While I waited I started to work on my long article in my mind. I wanted to start out with a short history of the abortion issue and I knew I had some research to do.

The wind picked up and I slumped farther down in the seat and watched the pale green branches of a weeping willow dance in the gusts. I noticed some movement and inched up so my eyes could see the Chasen residence over the steering wheel. The car in the driveway was backing up. As I watched, it pulled out into the street and Tom Chasen's familiar well-groomed head was recognizable. He drove away from me and I waited for five minutes before I got out of the car. I walked quickly and directly to the Chasen house. The dusk had sunk into dark gray and I didn't think anyone was watching from the neighboring ramblers.

I rang the doorbell, then waited a minute or so for Sandy to answer. She only opened the door a crack. Her hair was pulled back and her glasses were slipping down her nose. When she saw it was me she pushed the door open more and let me slip in the house. Holding her arms crossed over her chest, she looked at me with little recognition and then her eyes snapped into focus. "What are you doing here?"

"You called me."

"Yes, I know I called but I said to be careful. Didn't you understand?" She moved aside and let me come in. Her voice was whiney and monotone at the same time. I had heard pleasanter voices on horses.

"Well, it sounded important and I saw Tom drive away so I thought it was all right to come over."

She backed up into the house, looking at me as if I had something devious planned. "He's coming right back. He just went for milk. I'm not feeling very good. He says there's something wrong with me. I just don't know."

I peered out the door, but didn't see anyone coming. "So when would be good to meet?" I asked.

"Let's meet at the conservatory, the one in Como Park. I like to go there after I'm at the clinic. It makes me feel better. All those flowers." Her eyes lit up, then darkened as she added, "And Tom would never see us there."

"Great. When?"

"I can't tomorrow, but I think I can get away Tuesday.

139

Can you do it then?"

"Yes, fine. Tuesday. What time?"

"Let's say ten." She made it sound like we were making plans for brunch.

I heard a sound and then saw Sandy turn toward the door. "Oops," she said. The unmistakable sound of tires turning on cement announced Tom's arrival.

"Shit." The word popped out of me like a cork.

"You can't let him see you," Sandy said and leaned up against the wall, clutching her housecoat around her. Her face was chalky and she looked like she might pass out. "He'll know I've been talking. He warned me."

The car had stopped out front. I felt a fizziness in my head like I had gone too deep in water too fast. I needed to do something quick or he'd walk in on me. I looked around the hallway and then into the kitchen. "Is there a back door?"

"There's a door to the garage," Sandy started smoothing the front of her dress, "When he gets in, I'll get him into the kitchen and turn on the TV. Wait in the garage until you hear it come on loud and then sneak out."

"Yeah." I heard his footsteps on the walk and went where she pointed, through the kitchen to an entryway door. When I heard him opening the front door, I opened the back and slipped out.

I stood with my back to the door and strained to hear their conversation. It had happened so fast that I didn't have time to be afraid, but now, leaning against the door, I started to shake, an involuntary quivering that started at my shoulders and worked its way down my spine. I wanted to wait until Sandy got Tom settled in front of the TV, and I also wanted my eyes to adjust to the dark so I wouldn't bump into anything that would clatter and give me away.

The light from the street lamp shone in through the

long rectangular slits of window in the garage door. The light played across Sandy's car and a ladder on the far side of the garage.

I could hear them walking into the kitchen. Sandy's voice was like a piece of fine wire cutting through the air, while Tom's voice was more like the thunk of wood. I couldn't make out their words, but Sandy was doing most of the talking. I'm sure some adrenalin was pumping through her, too.

A pungent smell like vinegar tickled my nose. I cupped my hands around my nose and took slow shallow breaths. Don't sneeze, hold it another minute or two. When I was over the sneeze impulse, I looked around to see what was making the odor. My eyes were seeing more clearly now and leaning up against the side of the garage a few feet from me and the side door were pieces of flat wood cut in the shape of airplane propellers. The end three appeared to be covered with something. I took a couple careful steps and reached down to feel them. They had skins of fur stretched over them. I ran my hands down the skin and felt a long tail at the bottom. Sliding my hand over, I touched another skin with a tail. In my mind, I pictured squirrels scampering through tree-tops. What the hell was going on here?

The TV clicked on in the next room and I could hear the clock ticking for "Sixty Minutes." Not a moment too soon for me. I needed to get out of here. Walking slowly through the garage, I saw a snakelike hose that I stepped around and hoes and shovels that I stepped over. Sandy might be an avid gardener but she wasn't neat.

When I reached the door, I opened it a crack and looked out at Tom's car. All I needed to do was sprint down the driveway. The sound of the TV was louder. Morley Safer was going on about crime in the urban areas and I didn't want to be caught sneaking out of this Edina home. I pulled on the door and it flew open in my hands and I fell back, banging into a rake. Righting myself, I bolted through the door, pulled it shut and fled.

If Tom was going to check on the noise, he would do it immediately. When I got to my car, I slipped around the side of it and sat down on the curb out of sight. I didn't want to risk taking the time to get in the car. I heard the Chasens' door open and Sandy and Tom's voice arguing. Then the door slammed and I leaned my head against the side of my car door.

The night air was much cooler and I saw the stars were out. My overhead light was broken which for once was to my advantage. I got into the car, but slid down into the seat and didn't go anyplace. I didn't want Tom to notice a car pulling away. Glancing at my watch, I made myself wait another few minutes. Then I did it like in the movies. Start the car. Put it in gear. Check the street. Pull out slowly and drive away. After gliding down the block, turn the lights on.

I was worried about Sandy. She didn't look in good shape. Something was stirring her up pretty badly. I hoped she didn't break down and tell Tom I had stopped by. And I needed her to keep our appointment. I had to know what was going on. The feel of what I assumed were squirrel skins was still vibrating in my fingers. The line-up of skins meant there were more little squirrel carcasses, and I wondered if they were being stored in a freezer or if they had already been delivered to other women who had had abortions. Babies, squirrels, bombs —it wasn't a pretty picture.

16

FABIOLA LAY curled up in my lap as I drank a second cup of coffee. She looked like a furry pincushion. I stroked her back and swore she'd never be stretched into a hide like the squirrels I had seen yesterday. Furriers did use the fur of ferrets for coats, but they called it "fitch" from the Middle English word for ferret or polecat. When I first got Fab I read everything I could get my hands on about ferrets. It saved Fab's life that I did. Otherwise I wouldn't have known that once a female ferret goes into heat, she doesn't come out until she's impregnated. If this never happens, she gets anemic and dies. Fab was fixed as soon as she was old enough.

I hadn't called Dad on Sunday. I figured I'd give him and Christine a day together to see how they'd fall into place. But this morning I couldn't wait any longer and I called shortly after eight, wanting to talk while I was still home.

"Hi, Dad. How's it going?"

He said, "Fine," then paused. He cleared his throat and said, "You're calling awful early."

"Yeah, I thought I'd catch you before I left for work."

"Oh, yeah. So you're at home."

"Yes. How's everything going with Christine?"

"Fine. She made some oatmeal for breakfast this

morning. Haven't had oatmeal in a long time. Tasted kind of good."

It was hard work talking to my dad, because you had to read so much into so little. But since he was talking positively about the food, I decided I would use this as a barometer of how they were getting along. If he started to complain about her meatballs, I'd worry.

"Can I talk to Christine?"

"Sure." I heard him speak to her, "It's for you. Laura." I wondered if they were on a first name basis yet.

"Hi, Laura, it's going great." She sounded chipper, but I hoped she wasn't working hard at persuading herself and me that she was happy.

"You look around town?"

"Yeah, I went for a walk and in about a half an hour I figured I had seen the whole place."

"That sounds about right." I remembered how when I was growing up, one of my friends would get their parent's car, and we'd fill it with gas and then drive as far as we could for an hour or two, out into the prairie, just to get away from the small town that was starting to squeeze us to death.

"What's going on up there? Did you talk to the police or anyone?"

"Yes, I talked to Jarski and forensics determined positively that it was a squirrel. Actually I'm starting to wonder if you were the first woman to get a squirrel delivered to her. I'm going to do some checking on that today. There will be a piece in the newspaper about it today, but we're keeping your name out of it."

"Thanks."

"Listen, I usually check in with my dad a couple times of week, so I'll be in touch. Don't feel like I'm checking up on you and let me know if you need anything or if you're having any problems."

144

"He's quiet, your dad."

"Yes, he chooses his words carefully, but then he means them. He said the oatmeal tasted good."

"Oh, I'm glad he liked it."

Figured Dad wouldn't let her know that. "I'll talk to you soon."

"OK, thanks for calling."

* * *

At the office I wrote up the squirrel article. As I was reviewing it, Glynda stopped by and read it off the screen. She was wearing her shoulder-length hair pulled back and she actually looked quite elegant.

When she finished reading the piece, she handed it back to me and snorted. "God, next thing you know we're going to have the animal rights people up in arms. I think Jack should keep that in metro, second or third page. Let's not make a big deal about it, although it is interesting. You watch. I bet the wire service will pick it up. 'Skinned squirrel scares girl.' Try saying that a few times."

"We haven't gotten any more faxes, have we?"

"Nope, but I bet when your feature comes out we'll get some nasty letters."

"Maybe, but I am trying to cover all the angles in the abortion piece. I'm hoping that by showing all points of view, no one will complain. Course, if you try to please them all, you usually end up pleasing no one."

"How are you doing on on it?"

"I've got it laid out in my mind and I've done almost all the research. I think I'll start writing on Wednesday."

"If you don't mind, show it to me as it comes."

"OK, but it might come fast. I feel like this is one feature that'll come in one fell swoop."

Glynda had started to walk away when I said, "Like your hair like that."

145

She turned, doing a model pivot, and ran her hand over her hair. "You do? I think I'm going for a smoother look these days. More professional. But my husband doesn't like it. He likes it down. We'll see how it works." She winked and walked away. I wondered what it was supposed to work on.

I stayed in the office all morning and organized my thoughts. Forming the skeleton of my abortion feature, I read through my notes from interviews with Tom Chasen, Donna Asman, and Christine. I needed some more pro-life people. Maybe Meg Jameson—the Catholic viewpoint. I worked on the notes for a while and then my thoughts wandered to the bombing. I had tons of questions about Tom and Sandy Chasen and I knew one place I should check first.

I made a phone call and Gary picked up after the second ring.

"Hi," I started out tentatively.

"Well, this is a surprise." He waited.

"Yeah, I know. Sorry we didn't get to talk longer the other night, but it's a little hard for me right now. And I still do feel that what we've decided is best."

"What you've decided."

"Whatever."

"Why are you calling?"

"I need a favor, and it's a big one, and I know it."

"Shoot."

"Can you run a check on Sandy and Tom Chasen?"

"Laura, you don't ask for much, huh?"

"I know what I'm asking for but, don't worry, I won't use it inappropriately. I mean, I won't put it in an article or anything, unless I confirm it by some other means."

He was silent. Gary wasn't spontaneous. I didn't say anything. I knew what I was asking was a lot and it could get him into deep shit if it was found out.

"OK, stop by the station tonight on your way home. I'll try to have the info by then."

I said I would and when we hung up I wondered what strategy I was going to use to prevent Gary from asking me out and me from having to say no, when he had just done me this big favor.

B.T. wandered into my cubicle, pushed his butt onto my desk and sat there staring at me, his eyes dark like the end of a dull pencil. "So, how's it going?"

"Not bad. I'm working." Sometimes he needed to be told this.

"I see, you're slaving away, I can tell. Got time for a break?"

I pushed my notes away and looked up at him. He seemed a bit deflated as if he knew what needed to be done with the day, but didn't quite have the zip to do it. "Yeah, a few minutes chez Darlene's wouldn't hurt me."

We sat across from each other in our favorite booth, swung our jean-encased legs up on the seat, and leaned our backs against the wall. B.T. was trying to dress a little more stylishly now that he was seeing Josy and the results were not always favorable. Today he was wearing a plaid vest over his usual turtleneck and jeans and the vest looked like it had originally been used as a horse blanket. Maybe his cat had slept on it a few times. I kept wanting to pick hair off of it as we talked, but resisted. Darlene brought over two coffees without asking. Bless her, I thought.

"What'd you got that's sweet today?" B.T. asked.

"Blueberry muffins and caramel rolls."

B.T. looked at me, then back at Darlene, "I don't have the energy to unroll a caramel roll so bring me a muffin."

"Make it two." I looked at B.T. after Darlene had slouched away. "Are you all right?"

"Yeah," he said. "Just tired and out of ideas."

"Oh."

As we buttered and ate the muffins, I told him about the squirrel skins that I had discovered in the Chasen's garage.

"Should I tell Jarski about them?" I asked in conclusion.

"Why not?"

"Well, I feel like I should hear the whole story from Sandy or at least as much as I can get from her before I dump it in Jarski's lap."

"Fine, what're we talking about here, another day before you tell him? I don't think that's a big deal."

"Yeah, I hope it's not a big deal." I finished my muffin and folded up the wrapper into as small a package as I could. "Sandy Chasen's really scared about something, B.T. You should have seen her last night. I wonder if I'm just getting sucked into her paranoid world or if something is really going on."

B.T.'s eyes widened and his head sunk lower, a sign that he was worried. "Take care," he said. "No story's worth your life. An arm, perhaps."

"Yeah, yeah."

"OK. I have a question for you. I don't like the color they've painted the bridge over the freeway—the Armajani bridge—between Loring Park and the Walker. But I like the bridge. It's a cool bridge. I wish they would have just let it rust or something. But do you think that's enough to do a column on?"

"This question from the writer who managed to eke out fifteen inches on the new lights on the freeway? Who did two columns, not one but two, on the Christmas lights on the Foshay Tower? I think your architectural criticism is one of your strongest suits. I'm sure you're up to it."

"Thanks, Laura, I needed that."

"Are you going to talk about the lines of the poem?"

"You mean, painted on the bridge?"

"Yeah."

"No. I'll leave that for another column."

* * *

When B.T. and I got back in the office, I decided it was time to check on what did happen to fetal remains. Sandy's line about the babies was still haunting me and I wanted to be sure the Lifeliners weren't stockpiling fetuses someplace. I remembered when some members of a militant pro-life organization called Pro-Life Action Ministries raided a dumpster behind a family planning clinic in Robbinsdale and found twelve "aborted babies." There had been some legislation passed after that and I needed to find out what it was.

I called the library and had them pull all the clips they had on it. An hour later, they sent up the "paper clips"— yellowed clippings in envelopes. The legislature had passed a "fetal disposal law" and even though Planned Parenthood sought an injunction on the grounds that it was unconstitutional, the law was finally made official. It asked that the "human remains of an aborted or miscarried fetus be disposed of in a dignified manner, either burial or cremation."

Now, all I had to know was if the clinics were following the new law. I placed a call to Donna Asman and got through right away. She sounded busy so I launched right into the squirrel incident and asked if she had heard of anything like this happening before.

"Oh, god, how ghastly. What these people will do in the name of life. I don't get it. In answer to your question, I've heard of a number of incidents, but nothing like this before. Members of these anti-abortion groups take down the license plate numbers in our parking lot and do track some of these women home. Some of the women have gotten harassing phone calls. They've gotten hate mail.

But no midnight deliveries like this. Tell her I'm so sorry."

"Yes, I will." I glanced down at my notebook and looked at the many different ways I had written the next question. There was no graceful way of asking it so I plunged ahead. "I have one more thing I'd like to ask you. At your clinic, how do you dispose of the fetal remains?"

"Why?" She didn't sound surprised, more curious.

"I guess I want to be sure that women can only be delivered squirrels and not fetuses." It was the best I could do.

"Well, since the new law passed, we have found a funeral home which will handle the fetal remains. They cremate them."

"Thank you. I've written up the squirrel incident and it's coming out in the paper today. If you hear of anything related to it, please let me know or Detective Jarski."

"Certainly." She hung rather abruptly after that.

* * *

I entered the St. Paul police station, nodded at the officer behind the bulletproof plastic bubble, and took the elevator upstairs. I had been on the crime beat for four years and had spent more time in this place than my apartment some months. I wandered back to Gary's desk and he was entering something into his computer. His broad back was leaning forward and his hands bounced around when he typed.

"You look just like me," I said. "Writing up the latest news. Our jobs aren't so different."

"Have a chair," he nodded at the red vinyl-covered chair that had a pile of papers on it. I unloaded the pile and sat. He finished whatever he was typing and turned his attention to me.

"Nothing," he said.

"Damn."

"Not a thing. Clean, both of them."

It made sense but I had really been hoping that something would come up that would link Chasen with a prior bombing, or some such event. I thought for a second. When would he have been most apt to have gotten into trouble? When he was the young radical.

"OK, I want you to check one more person."

"Malloy," he sounded put upon, but interested.

"Chasen was married once before. Could you check her out for me?"

He looked around. "I can't do it now. I'm on my way out of here. But I will tomorrow."

I gave him the particulars on Sheila and thanked him. He didn't ask me out for a drink. Instead he told me what his wife was making him for dinner. Pot roast. It sure sounded good. I wished I had someone at home who was doing the same. So I left and even though I was relieved he hadn't asked me to do anything, in the oddest corner of my being I was sad. I had told him it was over and he had truly believed me. Maybe it was.

* * *

Since I was at the station, I decided to check in with Jarski. His partitioned-off office was a corner room with a window. It looked over a parking lot and the side of a tall building, but I'm sure that sometimes sunlight filtered its way down.

"A view and everything," I said as I walked in.

"Hey, don't I rate?" Jarksi looked up from the typewriter and gave a grimace. He was as neat as I'd ever seen him. But then I had to remember that the last time was at two in the morning. Now he was sporting a vest, a pin-striped shirt and a tie. And it was quite a tie. It reminded me of an Escher print—burgundy and navy boxes that ran

151

up and down it and turned into each other. Probably used it to confuse the criminals.

"What's new?" I asked and sat down in the only folding chair that wasn't covered with any old newspapers or folders.

"You should probably talk to Tennison, but they're moving. They've put together the explosive and it definitely was a pipe bomb. Forensics has been working day and night and they think they've assembled all the fragments. Now they're going to try hard to see whether they can pin anything on the Jameson kid. They had already searched his apartment but found zip there and now they're going to do his place of work tomorrow."

"You mean the wood stove store?"

"Yeah, geez, I'm sure they've got all the stuff to put a bomb together there. The squad's going to have their work cut out for them. Looking through all that sheet metal and all those tools." Jarski pulled out a file from a pile of them. "I've been through Robert Jameson's record though and boy, he's clean. He was actually a pretty good kid. Not super bright, but a hard worker. Nobody's had a bad word to say about him. I don't know. I think we might be barking up the wrong tree, but we gotta do it. It's just part of the post-blast investigation routine."

"How about the pro-life groups in town?"

"They're on the list. Don't worry. None of them have ever been too militant here in this town, but that doesn't mean they couldn't start. When the Supreme Court threw this issue back at the states, we should've ducked. It's going to bring on trouble and this might just be the beginning of it."

"I talked to Donna Asman today . . ."

He turned away from me and pulled at the paper in his typewriter, resituating it. "I know. She called. She was a little on edge. This is wearing her down I think. We're thinking of stationing a cop over there for a while. I think a lot of her workers are scared."

"And I'm seeing Sandy Chasen tomorrow. I'll let you know if I learn anything."

He started typing. "Yeah, fine, fine."

"Keep me posted." I got up to go. Jarski was obviously through with me.

He stopped typing and waved a hand at me. "I'll tell you what I can tell you. That's it, Malloy."

17

THE NIGHT WAS gentle and still. I was standing on the back deck of my apartment and staring at the sky. The deck faced west and the sun had gone down hours ago, but that was the direction our weather came from and all I could see was velvet-deep sky and smatterings of stars.

It was moving on toward May and I was a believer again. Summer and basking warm weather was actually going to make it to Minnesota. There were days in mid-January when it was twenty-five below, with a windchill of minus fifty and it seemed that we would all be captured in permafrost. But all around me there were signs of growth. Fringes on the trees, lime-green fronds pushing up from the earth. And I could feel it in myself. My shoulders unhunched, my skin smoothed out, my hair took on some buoyancy.

The phone rang in the house and I reluctantly left the view and the sweet softness in the air to go back inside. I heard it ring again and tried to remember where I had left it. That was a problem with the portable phones; they could get lost. Moving toward the sound, I located it next to the couch, answered it, then plunked down in the corner of the couch.

"Yes," I said.

"This Laura?" a male voice asked.

"Yes, it is. Who's this?"

"Paul. I'm just down the block. Can I come by? I need to talk to someone."

He sounded winded or worse. "I guess. I'll be here."

He hung up and so did I. Wondering why I had agreed to this visit, I looked down at myself. I had gotten ready for bed and was wearing an old white cotton slip and that's all. I ran to my bedroom, pulled off the slip, buttoned on an old oxford, pulled on some jeans, slipped into espadrilles, combed my hair. Ran to the bathroom and brushed my teeth. Threw Fabiola into her room. The doorbell rang.

I skidded down the stairs, stopped for a moment at the bottom, then let him in. Backing up one stair, I was slightly taller than he was. Paul didn't look like he was in good shape. His blue eyes swam in slightly blood-shot whites, his black hair was raked back from his forehead. He had a denim jacket on over black jeans.

"What's going on?" I asked.

"Hey, I'm sorry to barge in on you like this, but I needed to talk to you. See, I don't know what's going on. I stopped down at Dick Tracy's and had a few shots of whiskey. Get up my courage or get me through this. But I wanted to come and see you."

I could sense the liquor in him. His body swayed like it was floating on water, and his eyelids drooped. He was talking slow, so as not to stumble over words. He was drunk, but sober enough to know it. I wondered how many last shots he had had before coming over.

"Can you make it up the stairs?" I backed up a few more steps, giving him some space.

"Oh, sure, no I'm fine, not like that. I'm just a little bit over the line, not much." While talking he attempted to located the first step with his foot, but didn't have much luck. Once he stopped talking and set his whole mind to it,

155

he found the step and then the next. I kept backing up, but didn't get too far away, in case he lost his footing. Once upstairs I led him to the couch.

"How about a cup of coffee?" I didn't sit, but asked him standing so I could continue on into the kitchen.

"Do you have any beer?" he asked.

"Nope, and I wouldn't give you any if I did. But a cup of coffee might do you some good. Do you have a ride home?"

"My car's down the street. I'm staying at my mom's these days. Keep her company," he said and looked around the room as if he were surfacing for a moment. "Nice place."

"Thanks. I'll put some water on and be right back." In the kitchen I filled my kettle full of water and put it on the stove. I thought back to my conversation with Jarski and wondered if the police had already talked to Paul.

When I walked back into the living room, he was leaning forward, holding his head. I sat down on the other end of the couch from him and nudged him with my foot. "What's going on with you? What're you doing over here?" I asked.

He lifted his head up and stared off past me, then looked straight ahead and spoke to the room, "I didn't know who else to talk to. You know all about what's going on—the bomb, Bobby. Somehow I think you could tell me what to do."

He paused, licked his lips nervously and continued, "I got some visitors today and they asked a lot of questions and I told them where to go. I don't think they appreciated me. They said they're coming back tomorrow with a search warrant."

"You sent them away?" Tennison didn't like to be crossed. Paul was asking for big trouble. Now they'd really do a number on his place.

"Yup."

"That wasn't very smart."

"Shit, they're threatening to tear my place apart. They're looking for evidence to blame this bomb shit on Bobby. What am I supposed to do, help them out? Man, it burns me up. It should be against the law."

"Listen, Paul, they are the law." I knew it didn't do much good to try to explain anything to a drunk, but maybe he would hear and remember a little of what I said. "They are only checking out your place because Bobby had access to all the tools there. The sooner they go through your place and don't find anything, the sooner they'll start checking out in earnest the other possibilities. For example, the pro-life groups that have been threatening and picketing the clinic."

"OK, I hear you." He took off his jacket and bundled it up. "But what if they do find something?"

"Then they'll look at Bobby more closely and there's nothing you can do about that."

"This is all my fault. I should have taken care of Bobby. I shouldn't have let him go with Christine."

"You're only his brother, not his keeper. You did a lot for him. You gave him work and you listened to him. Who could do more than that? Give yourself a break."

The kettle whistle blew in the next room. "It'll take me a few minutes to make the coffee. Just relax."

I decided I'd have a cup too. It was past eleven and past my bedtime. If I was going to have to stay up until Paul was sober enough to go home, I'd need some help doing that. I ground some French roast beans and put them in my Melitta. A dash of water to cover the grounds, and then slowly pour it in and through. I loved the smell of it. I made a potful and poured out two cups and headed back into the living room.

There I found a sacked-out Paul. His head was tilted

157

straight back on the couch, his mouth open, and his strong neck exposed. His hands were folded in his lap and he looked like a young boy who had fallen asleep in church. Unknowing and uncaring. Sleep would be the best thing in the world for him. Much better than coffee. I got a spare pillow and slid it under him, tilting him sideways on it. He nestled into it and then I threw an afghan over him.

Running my hand over the patterned gold and orange daisies, I remembered when my mother had crocheted it for me several Christmases ago. It gave me comfort to snuggle under it, maybe it would help Paul a little. I needed to call his mother and let her know he was here.

* * *

Meg Jameson insisted on coming over to get her son. I decided to let him sleep until she came. His head had fallen sideways and he was snoring, but he wasn't bothering me. I sat down on the floor of the living room and went back to work on my books. I had finished the fiction section and it took up half the wall of shelves.

Starting on the nonfiction, I was faced with the decision of how to arrange them—alphabetically or by subject matter? I was leaning toward subject matter, but then I ran into the basic problem of how to determine what a book was about. For example, Natalie Goldberg's *Wild Mind*— was it women's studies, writing, or self-help or even autobiography? I'd bought it as a writing book so I decided to put it in that pile.

Paul started to turn on the couch and I stood up, ready to catch him if he rolled off, but he didn't. I walked over and sat down in the vinyl easy chair next to him. I had bought the chair at a used office supply store and I liked it because you could spill coffee on it or curl your feet up into it without worry.

I stared at Paul. His face was in profile against the pillow. Nice nose, long eyelashes and full lips. I felt sorry for him and all that had happened to him, but didn't admire him for falling apart. And yet, I felt the tiniest bit of lust for him. It was a small feeling, but I nodded to it as it came in and out of my thoughts. Paul was good-looking in the dark, sorrowful way that I liked, successful in his business, and in need. Actually, the "in need" part worked against him. I didn't want him to come knocking on my door drunk again. At the bar and again tonight, I felt like he wanted some kind of absolution from me, or blessing.

The neighing doorbell went off and Paul jerked awake. He stared around in alarm, his eyes squinting at me.

"I called your mom," I explained and went downstairs to let her in.

Meg Jameson was standing up straight, chin high, facing my door. Her hair was a white cloud around her head and she held onto her purse with both hands. Probably didn't like this neighborhood. She was wearing a spring coat, a piece of apparel most women didn't own anymore, and nylons. I assumed a dress was under the coat. I let her in and thanked her for coming.

"Oh, no. I should be thanking you for calling me. I was getting worried about Paul. I've been so worried about him. Thank you so much."

I didn't want to argue about who should thank whom so I accepted hers and led her up the stairs. Paul was actually standing up next to the couch and said hi to Meg. Then he looked at me and asked where the bathroom was. I didn't like the hue of his face. He looked like he was feeling ill.

I pointed and he headed in the right direction, walking with only a slight tilt to his gait. I thought he might be a while and offered to take Meg's coat.

"That's all right. I'm fine."

"Would you like a cup of coffee?" I asked, remembering the pot I had brewed for Paul. If I zapped a couple cups in the microwave, it would be drinkable.

"Yes, please. I take cream and sugar."

When I brought out a tray with two cups of coffee and the neccessary condiments and a plate of Fig Newtons, I found Meg perched on the edge of the couch. I placed everything in front of her, helped myself to coffee and settled into my chair. She followed my lead and managed to slide back on the couch and look more comfortable.

"Do you live here all alone?" she asked. She looked down at the piles of books on the floor.

"No, I have a ferret."

"Oh, a ferret. So you're not married?"

"No." I felt like the "no" all by itself was a little blunt, but I didn't know how to soften it.

"Well, I expect with your job you keep awfully busy, don't have much time to cook or keep house."

"No and I'm not much interested either."

Meg swallowed some coffee and picked up a cookie. "I don't often have store-bought cookies. I always bake."

"I bake snickerdoodles," I told her, not to be outdone.

"Oh, Bobby always liked those." Her face darkened and then she looked right at me. "I still can't believe he's dead, that he's not going to come strolling through the kitchen door and ask what's for dinner. That damned Christine, it's all her fault."

"Bobby was in on the decision, after all he went with her." Why was I bothering to argue with her? She was in pain and needed to blame it on someone.

"For God's sake, why didn't she just have the baby?" Meg was leaning forward and stirring her coffee, wildly. Her already wrinkled face was furrowed in pain.

I thought for a second. She should ask Christine. It wasn't up to me to explain Christine's decision. But I could help her along. "She's only nineteen. She wanted a better life. I get that."

"I was nineteen when I had my first child. I had no choice. Had to get married. But I love my kids. I can't imagine doing what she's done. It goes against the grain of being a woman." Meg took a sip of her coffee, shaking her head. "I would have raised the kid if she hadn't wanted it. I would have done anything to keep my Bobby alive."

Meg pursed her lips. She opened her purse, then looked at me.

"I don't mind if you smoke," I said.

She pulled out a pack of Virginia Slims and lit up. "I'm so worried about my Paul. I've never seen him such a wreck. Won't go to confession. Hardly eats. He wasn't like this when his father died. He was a real little man then. Helped me like you wouldn't have believed. I rely on him so. He's the best son. Always thinks of me."

I didn't say anything. I remembered Paul talking about his father's death and how he had felt relieved by it.

Meg continued on, "Bobby was a real charmer, but you couldn't count on him. But now Paul, he's responsible. He knows the way things should be." She smoked in short little bursts, puffing and then spitting the smoke out. Maybe she was trying not to inhale.

She crushed her cigarette out in the old cowboy hat ashtray I had sitting on the coffee table. "I wonder if Paul's all right. I'm going to go check."

I stayed put. I heard Meg knock on the bathroom door and then heard the low rasp of Paul's voice answering. I was beginning to see why Paul was who he was. His bond to his mother was so strong that it must be hard to try to find a woman to replace her. Why was she even here? She should have told me to put him in a cab and then let him in when he made it home. Family dynamics were so bizarre.

Paul came staggering out of the bathroom and Meg held him up. Paul was saying, "Mom, I'm sorry. You

161

didn't have to come."

"Let's get you home," she crooned to him. Her arm was around his back, she was almost carrying him. She was a tall woman and he was leaning heavily on her so their heads were close together. The hallway light shone on her white hair and made it a halo, his slicked back hair and deep eyes made him appear so much darker than Meg. The two of them formed a kind of Pietà and I was touched by it, even if I didn't understand what went on between them. What would they do for each other?

18

I THINK I'VE got what you want," Gary said, then paused. I was still trying to remember what I wanted when Gary went on. My eyes wouldn't come open and somehow I had found the phone with my flailing hand. "Good," I said, stalling.

"So, Malloy, late night?"

It had been. Paul and Meg had left about twelve-thirty and there I was sitting on the couch, all wired up from a big cup of coffee and with enough emotional energy in me to talk someone's ear off. So instead I worked on the nonfiction section of my library until two in the morning. I had set the alarm for seven-thirty but obviously had paid no attention to it. It was now eight o'clock and I knew Gary was in at the police station already. He was a morning person, liked to clear his desk before noon when he worked the morning shift.

"Thanks for calling, Gary. Yeah, but nothing exciting. Just trying to set my life in order." I stood up and aimed myself toward the kitchen. A cup of coffee was the only answer.

"Oh, one of those."

The sun was hitting the dishes in the sink, the cups we had drank coffee out of. I sat at the table and stared at the streaks of dust on my windows and waited for Gary to say something.

"Well," Gary sounded impatient.

Then I realized he was waiting for me to respond to his opening salvo. "What? Something on Sheila?"

"Yeah. I got a copy of her police file this morning. The whole thing—arrests, but no convictions. She was arrested a couple times in 1970. First time for disturbing the peace. No big deal, the charges were dropped. But the second time it was for a bombing that took place at the ROTC building on the U of M campus. Do you remember that?"

Where was a piece of paper? I needed to get this down. I scrambled and found an old ballpoint pen under a newspaper on the table and starting writing on a flyer for two dollars off a pizza. "I remember there was stuff going on at the U, but I was only fifteen."

"The deal was someone set a bomb off in the entryway. It was a pipe bomb, not too big. Nobody was hurt when it went off, but it made a mess of a couple doors. She was found in the building at the time and arrested, but later let go. Lack of evidence. She claimed she had nothing to do with it. It was suspected she belonged to a militant anti-war group, the SDS."

Shit, I thought. The time was right. She was with Tom then. He might well have had something to do with it. I wondered if that was how he worked. He made the bombs and got the women to deliver them. *Burros*, that's what they called women when they carried drugs. I had an image of a young Sheila, dressed in a flowing flowered hippie dress with a pipe bomb tucked underneath, looking like a pregnant woman, delivering a stick of death. "I do remember that group. SDS, didn't it stand for Students for a Democratic Society? There was talk of them at my high school."

164

"That's it. That's her whole record. Never arrested since."

"Thank you. This is great. It could mean something." I stopped, as I knew I had to reassure him. "Listen, Gary. I really appreciate this. And in no way will I let anyone know that you got this info for me. Now that I know this bombing incident took place I can look it up in our files, get the articles written on it. That way I can safely pass it on to Tennison. I would never jeopardize you in any way."

"Yeah, I'm not worried. I know I can trust you." His voice dropped down a notch and he spoke as if he didn't want to be overheard. Maybe someone was walking by his desk. "Listen, Laura. I can't do stuff like this for you anymore. I'm cleaning up my act and I need to not talk to you for a while. I'm trying to make my marriage work again."

It was the same decision I had come to, to clean up my act. But it was always harder to hear it thrown back at you. I didn't want to need Gary, but I didn't want him to get over me so fast. He had provided excitement in my life, certainly, but he was a friend too. He understood how I'd get zipped up on whatever I was working on. He said I was like an intellectual cop. I went after the bad guys in words, he did it with a gun. There was something to that. So we had connected on several levels, but lately all we seemed to be doing was saying goodbye.

"Hope it works, Gary. I'm pulling for you. Thanks and all."

"Yeah, I'll be reading you."

* * *

I made it in before eight-thirty. The few times I did come in this early, I liked it. There were people around working, but it wasn't frantic like it would get as deadline approached mid-morning. A steady hum filled the air, the

165

clack of keyboards fingered and thoughts running across screens. I grabbed a cup of coffee from the conference room and slid behind my desk without bumping in to anyone.

In passing, I noticed that B.T.'s cubicle was deserted. I wanted to talk to him about what had happened last night and to tell him how lucky he was that I hadn't called him at one in the morning. I hoped B.T. got in before I had to leave to meet Sandy.

I walked down to the library and had them pull anything on the bomb incident at the ROTC building, but, scanning the copy, I found no mention of Sheila's name. Because they hadn't pressed charges against her, it might never have come out in the paper. How was I going to get that information in a way that I could safely pass on to Tennison? He needed to know that Tom Chasen could have been involved in a past bombing. I remembered how friendly and talkative Sheila had been and decided maybe I needed some more flowers for my home. The lilacs hadn't lasted long.

On my way back, I circled past B.T.'s cubbyhole and saw he had made it in. "Hi."

He looked up, surprised. His forehead wrinkled over like a wind had blown across water and then came clean when he smiled at me. His desk looked like someone had broken into the newsroom in the middle of the night and had rifled through his papers digging for something, but it was just the way B.T. structured order—chaotically. He said he was deep into chaos theory: "If it worked for physics, why not for me." He actually did have a heavy tome about chaos on his desk, but he mainly used it as a paper weight. "Pretty ding-dang early for you, Laura. What're you working on?"

"The latest trend—baby bombers."

"Ow, that's horrible." He winced, then pointed at two

styrofoam cups of coffee on his desk. "You want one?"

"Naw, I had a couple cups early this morning. I'm going to wait a while."

"What were you doing up so early? Very unlike you." He sipped his coffee cautiously, while keeping his eye on me.

I shrugged my shoulders. "I had visitors last night." And I preceded to tell him about Paul and Meg.

At the end, he unfolded a napkin and blew his nose in a melodramatic way. "Well, if she's anti-abortion, my guess is that momma's boy is anti-abortion too."

"Oh, I think that's true. I wonder what the police will find at his shop. He wouldn't be dumb enough to have anything there if he was involved with the bomb. Although he didn't expect it to be traced to his brother. I don't know."

Then I told him about the information I had gotten on Sheila. B.T. was twirling back and forth in his office chair as I was speaking. At first it was a habit I hated, but now I was used to turning my head back and forth and it helped me loosen up my shoulders, which I tended to hunch up when I worked at my terminal.

"Great stuff. But what's the matter? You seem a little down."

"Well, Gary called and he doesn't want to see me anymore."

"But that's good. That's what you want, right? He's listening to you."

"Yeah, I guess but I thought he'd mourn a little longer."

"But that's how married men mourn. They go back to their wives."

"B.T., you're brutal."

"Laranemo, that's what our relationship is made up of—poking and prying. It's called caring."

167

I decided it was time to give him a little of his own. "So how's the other mother in your life?"

B.T. turned a little sheepish. "Well, I'm going to meet the other man in Josy's life on Thursday. We're all going out for pizza."

"That sounds nice."

"Yeah, I like pizza. But I bet this kid won't like olives or anchovies on it. I was thinking I'd bring him something. Do you think a five-year-old American boy would like a baseball signed by Harmon Killebrew?"

"He won't know who Harmon Killebrew is, but he'll like the ball, I'm sure."

"I'm going to think about it. I'd hate to throw away a good baseball like that on a kid who wouldn't appreciate it. Maybe I should wait and see what he's like."

From where I was standing in B.T.'s cubicle I could see down the hallway to the elevators. When I looked down it after his last comment I saw a man with thin blond hair and aviator glasses get off the elevator and look around. He was holding an attaché case and as he turned to look toward me, I ducked back into B.T.'s cubicle.

"Listen, I need your help. Tom Chasen is here. I'm meeting his wife in fifteen minutes. I want to see what he's got on his mind, but it can't take too long. I'm going down to my desk and would you come and interrupt us in about five minutes and say we have a meeting?"

"Gotcha." B.T. slammed the file cabinet drawer shut and winked.

I snuck back to my desk and proceeded to look very busy. After a moment, I could feel someone standing behind me. I spun around and Tom Chasen appeared startled, then gathered himself together. He was holding his attaché case like a shield in front of his groin area and I realized he was not sure how to handle me.

"Miss Malloy, Tom Chasen."

I sat up straight and clicked my pen. "Yes, how can I help you?"

"Sorry to disturb you at work, but it was on my way." He cleared his throat, then looked around for a chair. I decided to keep him standing, so I didn't unfold the one that was leaning next to my computer. "My wife has mentioned your name several times and I'm afraid she might try to contact you again."

"Fine. I'm working on this piece about the abortion issue and I'd be delighted to hear from her."

"Well, no. Please don't talk to her. If she should do so, I would like you to get in touch with me. She hasn't been feeling well and I am trying to do all I can to help her, but. . . ." He stopped for a minute and I could feel him weighing what he could tell me. "She imagines things sometimes and I wouldn't want her imaginings to get out. It could be embarrassing for many people. Do you understand?"

"No, Mr. Chasen. Like what?"

He finally decided to set down his attaché case, but then he wasn't sure what to do with his hands. He pushed his case in front of him and moved in on me, his voice getting lower. "I can't go into it. It's a private matter and that is what it must remain. Do I have to put it more clearly?"

"I do understand that you don't want me to speak with your wife, but I don't understand why." I decided it was time to switch the subject. I was certainly giving him no promises of any sort. "Last time we spoke, I asked you to check around and see if anyone in your organization had any information about the bombing at the clinic last week. Did you come up with anything?"

"Nothing. We had a meeting at the office and in fact people were quite concerned. Bombs are not the way we work. We have most of the people of this state behind us and we don't need to resort to such maneuvers." He stood up straighter as he spoke and it sounded as if he had slipped into a short segment of a speech. On this subject, he felt on solid ground.

I decided to pull the rug out from under him. "Did you in the past ever work with explosives?"

"Where do you get off asking me such a thing?" He spit the words out. Finally I was seeing a little emotion from him.

"I was just reading about a bombing that happened at the University in 1970. Wasn't that around the time you were active in the anti-war movement?"

"Who have you been talking to?" His face had blanched.

"Mr. Chasen, this is public knowledge. I didn't have to dig very deep to find out your past."

"I'm warning you Miss Malloy, stay away from me. Stay away from my wife. You don't know what you're playing with."

"Are you threatening me?"

He reined himself in. "No, of course not. I'm concerned about my wife's well-being and I'm asking for a little consideration."

B.T. bombed in at that moment. "Hey, Laura, get your butt in gear. Meeting in three seconds. Excuse me. Didn't mean to interrupt anything." Then he sped out.

"I have to go," I said to Chasen, standing up and grabbing my notebook and jacket.

He took a step in closer to me and said through tight-pressed lips, "Leave us alone. I'm warning you. You don't know what you're getting into, Miss Malloy."

"I have a job to do, Mr. Chasen. I write stories about what goes on in this world. You might not like them, especially not the endings, but it's my work." I swept around him and walked down the hall toward the back stairwell.

170

19

I HADN'T BEEN to the Conservatory at Como Park since I was in sixth grade and my school from Waseca came up for a field trip. I remembered that trip as I parked down the street from the large greenhouse structure. It had been a snowy day, but inside the Conservatory it was summer, a jungle of flowers and hanging vines and best of all humidity, something we didn't get in Minnesota in the winter. I had dreamed of sneaking away from my class and hiding in a corner behind a palm tree until everyone was gone. I had wanted a few hours alone in paradise. I wondered what I would think of it now.

The tall dome of the Conservatory shone in the morning sun and through the steamy glass windows I could see palm fronds. Looking up at the green leaves pushing against the glass, trying to get out to the sun, I wondered if they felt trapped in there.

I watched the door, thinking I might see Sandy go in or thinking she might already be in there waiting for me. I was reminded of how I felt when I left a bowl of chili in my refrigerator too long and was afraid of what I might find when I took the tin foil off of it. I knew I had to ask Sandy some questions, but I was dreading her answers.

The air inside the Conservatory was moist and tropical. There were birds flying around inside and as I walked

171

around the first path, a drop of water fell on my shoulder. I looked up and saw the steaminess of the air condensing on the inside of the cooler glass panes. So it rained in here. A thermometer on a tree read seventy-nine degrees. My suitcoat felt heavy so I took it off and rolled up the sleeves of my shirt.

Looking for Sandy, I walked all around the Conservatory. It consisted of the main room under the dome and two side wings—the fern room and the bonsai room. Moosehead ferns, plants I had only seen in pots, looked the way they might grow in the wild. I remembered a trip to Washington D.C., how astonished I had been to see ivy actually growing in lawns.

After circling the whole place, I settled in the middle of the main room, where I could see the door. There were two cement benches around a fountain. "Crest of the Wave," constructed in 1925, a placard read. It was a sculpture of a nude woman, her arms thrown high, walking in amongst waves and fish, done by Harriet W. Frishmuth. Around me, orchids were blooming, a purple that was so intense it seemed artificial, and above them bird-of-paradise, offering orange lips with a blue dagger tongue.

It was a quarter after ten and I was getting nervous, but there was nothing I could do. I couldn't call Sandy and see if she was home. She was supposed to be coming from the clinic so that wouldn't do any good. Tom hadn't said anything about restricting her to the house. Even though she hadn't looked very well the other night, when he talked of her "sickness" I didn't get the impression he meant strep throat or the flu.

I went and stood by the fountain and watched the water squirt out of the fishes' mouths in a ring around the nymphet. Over the years, she had turned a light blue streaked-bronze color and seemed happy. It was nice to see women's art celebrating women in a public place.

172

Turning my back to the fountain I leaned against the fountain rim and thought about what I needed to get out of Sandy. First, figure out what the reference to the babies meant. Second, ask her about the squirrels. And, third, the bomb. See what she knew about the bomb at the clinic. Just, please, let her show up.

"This is a good spot," Sandy tapped me on the shoulder and I jumped. When I turned quickly to look at her, she was nodding her head, and I tried not to let her see that she had startled me.

"Should we sit down here?" I pointed back to the bench.

"Yes, I like it with the water. No one can overhear us. Although I've been thinking I might have to go public with this information."

"What exactly are you talking about?" I looked her over carefully. Today she was the essence of neatness and blandness. Tan overcoat unbuttoned, cream-colored polyester shirt with a bow at the collar, brown skirt that hit right below the knee, and skin-colored nylons that always looked a little orangey to me. Her eyes were hidden behind her glasses, but in this bright light I was able to make out their color—a murky brown. I wanted to pick an orchid and put it in her hair, give her some color.

She wiped the bench with a handkerchief she pulled out of her coat pocket and then sat on the edge of it. "I've been planning how I would tell you this, so you have to let me do it my way."

I could tell she had rehearsed this, but I let her continue. She turned her face to me and it seemed to have taken on a glow. She was smiling as she announced, "Woman are meant to be mothers. Mary, the virgin, was a mother. See how important it is. Where would we be if Mary had decided not to be a mother? God comes out through us in our children. Men think they get us preg-

173

nant, but often it's really God. He comes to us in the night and lays down with us."

Yikes, I thought. I had had a friend whose mother had thought she was the Virgin Mary and Sandy was moving in close to that territory. As I recalled, they put my friend's mom on lithium. "Has this happened to you?"

"I'm not at that part yet." She was irritated with me for interrupting. "So you see that's why the killing must be stopped because many of those children are God's children. They must be protected and allowed to grow up. They will bring us great goodness and mercy. It's all in the Bible. Have you read the Bible?"

"Yes, I've read it."

"Good, then you can understand. I've always felt you could understand, that you knew how important this all is. Tom doesn't understand that each child is important. That no matter where they came from, they must be allowed to come into the world. Even if it is difficult on the mother. He has been killing babies too. And he goes out into the world and acts so clean and good. But he's not."

Her face started to crumple, to fall in on itself. "He's like all the rest. He has made me kill babies and I fought it. I tried so hard. . . ." She started to cry and I was glad for the soothing cover of the waterfall. A soft sob rose out of her and her shoulders hunched and jerked.

I spoke softly. I wanted the information to keep coming. "What do you mean he killed babies? Where did he get them? Did he have help?"

"I hate him. I know I'm supposed to love him, but sometimes I hate him. They were mine. They were given to me by God. Divine conception. They would be walking now. They would be talking and one would be reading. One would be three and the other one year old. I miss them so much." She started to cry louder.

I looked around. No one was paying any attention to

174

us. Patting her shoulder, I said that I bet she missed them. But I needed to know what she was talking about. "Sandy, this is real important. What do you mean when you say that Tom's been killing babies? You've got to explain."

She stopped crying rather suddenly, as if she had changed course in a storm. When she looked up at me, her face was hardened. "I'll tell you everything when I'm ready. I need to be sure you'll handle my information in a good way. I want you to help me write an article for the paper."

I thought quickly. She wanted to write for the paper. It would have to be a letter to the editor and then we wouldn't have to print it, depending on what she said. "Yes, I think that's a good idea. In the form of a letter. Can you give me some kind of idea as to what Tom has been doing? More specifically."

She shook her head as she looked at me. "Don't you get it. Don't you hear what I'm saying. He's been killing my babies. What's the matter with you?" She leaned toward me and was close to screaming at me.

I decided to change the subject for a moment and try to get her to calm down that way. "What have you been doing with the squirrels? I noticed the skins in your garage."

She brightened noticeably. "The squirrels. I go out and shoot them. When I was a child, my dad would take me squirrel hunting. I skin them and then I wash them and pretend they're my babies. When the baby is five months old in the womb, it's the size of a baby squirrel. Did you know that?"

"Have you given any of them away?"

"If only the women could see their babies, they would never get rid of them. I'm only trying to help them. The next time they won't do it. They'll remember what their babies looked like and they won't kill their babies again."

175

I was starting to get a picture of what was going on inside her mind. Now, I had to see how far she would go with her plans to reform the women of the world. "What about the bomb, Sandy? You know, the bomb that went off at the clinic last week? Was that part of your plan?"

"Yes, I was there. The bomb, that was the wrath of God. He works in mysterious ways. I'm sure it has stopped some women from coming to the clinic. I have other plans. You'll see. I will let you know." She grabbed my arm. "The reason I'm talking to you is . . . if it's printed up in the paper, it will reach everyone that way."

"Sandy, did you have anything to do with the bomb?"

She wiped her face with her hands, pulling them straight down her cheeks. A woman with a mission, she was gathering herself together. "I will tell you what to write. I don't want to talk about bombs. They are only a means to an end. The real issue is that all babies are gifts from God. It's that simple. Do you understand? Can you write my message?"

I nodded my head encouragingly, but what I said was more noncommital. "I'll have to check with my editor."

"You have to do this. It is of infinite importance. I have more to say to you, but I need to go grocery shopping now. I always do the shopping on Tuesdays." She was standing up, straightening her coat, and looked like she was ready to leave.

Her quick about-face to shopping had me spinning. I grabbed her arm. "Let's talk more. Can you give me a few more minutes?"

"Not right now." She looked at her watch. "Tom will be home for lunch soon. I need to go shopping."

"Call me later." I said. "Sandy, you call me if you're going to do anything." I gave her another card with my home number and my work number. "Call any time. Just

176

like you did last time. I'll get back to you. Leave a message if you have to."

"I might do something. I'm waiting for God to tell me what to do. Who knows...." She rubbed her stomach. "He might give me another baby. And this time I won't tell anyone. I'll keep it a secret and when it is born, everyone will see the power and the glory that is His."

She waved as she left and I sat back down on the bench. I was overwhelmed by her—she would flip in and out of herself and this other character, the woman of God. I wondered if she was a split-personality, or merely psychotic, or a saint. What were the differences? Point of view. And she hadn't really told me anything concrete. She seemed to have her own message and whenever I had tried to break in with questions, I would throw her off track.

I still wasn't sure what she meant when she said that Tom had killed her babies. He didn't want me to talk to Sandy so maybe I could use that as a lever to get information out of him.

As I was leaving, I saw a banana tree by the door. I had never seen one before and I let my eyes wander over it, the large leaves like the green ears of an elephant, the buds of bananas, tight as a fist and green, but pointing sunward. This was news to me, bunches of bananas didn't hang down toward the ground, but pointed up to the sun and slowly turned yellow if they were allowed to stay on the tree. The assumptions we make. I wondered what I was assuming about Sandy Chasen. Her babies might be nothing, made up, they might be kernels that were in her body, they might be other women's children that she adopted in her mind.

I was still in a quandary over what to do with the information I was getting. It certainly wasn't right for a story. If Sandy was mentally tilting, I didn't want to expose her to the public eye. But if she had had something to do with the bombing, I needed to let Tennison and Jarski know.

* * *

I went back to the office and worked on my article, but I kept thinking about Sandy. I felt like she was dangerous and yet I didn't know how to stop her. One possibility was that she had admitted to me that she had skinned the squirrels. I wondered what the charge would be for leaving a skinned squirrel at someone's doorstep. It didn't really matter. I just needed to get the police to be aware of her and at the same time let her know that she was being watched. What she really needed was psychiatric help.

I tried to call Jarski, but he was out of the office. I didn't bother with Tennison, because I knew where he was—at Paul's store. My eyes drifted up to one of the postcards I had pinned to the wall in front of me—the south of France—and I imagined going there in the fall, eating moules in a small café, drinking a deep, red Beaujolais, smelling lavender, meeting some wonderful man. I had to laugh at myself. It was so typical. I could never imagine being with a man in my life, the way it actually took place. I always had to transport romance to some place magical, some place outside of the world I lived in. Trying to make undressed beds, cold suppers, hairs in the bathtub romantic was too hard for me.

* * *

Walking into the flower shop, I smelled the same warm humid air that had been in the Conservatory. Tom's ex-wife and Sandy had some things in common. They both loved flowers and they both wanted babies. A certain fecundity about them, although Sheila looked more bounti-

178

ful. I saw her leaning over a large vase of roses and burying her nose in it.

"How do they smell?" I asked.

"Wonderful," she laughed as she stood up. "Actually they remind me of Tang, you know, that orange drink the astronauts took to the moon."

"Let me smell."

She brought a single rose over to me, a long-stemmed peach-colored rose. One large inhalation confirmed her analysis of the aroma. "That's Tang all right. But a little more refined."

"What can I help you with?" she asked, wiping her hands on her white apron. It was over a dress that had a yellow background with small bouquets of pink flowers. Her hair was halfway down her back, gathered together at the very end in a loose ponytail that was held together with a wire. "Oh, I remember you. You came in last week, asking about Tom. You're a writer for the paper, right? What's your name again?"

"Laura Malloy."

"Oh, yes, I remember now." she said and still looked glad to see me. "You were writing that piece on the abortion issue. Are you done with it?"

"Not quite." I was getting ready to launch into my questions when she interrupted me.

"Well, I have great news," she announced. Smiling so her large blue eyes curved into almond shapes, she said, "I found out yesterday—I'm pregnant."

"Great," I said, feeling a jolt of joy for her.

"I'm telling everyone. I'm so happy. I just found out yesterday. I think I told you I was trying in vitro. Well, I really lucked out. First time and it took. And they're pretty sure that there is only one fetus. God, twins, can you imagine." She rubbed her apron over her stomach. "Only five weeks along, but I can tell. I was pretty sure.

179

I've been feeling so sleepy."

"Congratulations," I leaned on the counter. She made pregnancy look easy. "I had a few more questions about Tom. The time when you were together."

"I was thinking a lot about that after you left. I wasn't sure yet if I was pregnant and I remembered back to when he and I were trying. How disappointed I'd feel each month. After we broke up, I wondered if he had problems, you know, if he was sterile or something. But his mother told me that Sandy, his wife, was pregnant a year ago. I don't know what happened though. They didn't have a kid, did they?"

"No, they didn't. Sandy was pregnant, huh? I hadn't heard about that." I didn't know how I was going to get to the bottom of what was going on with Sandy, it got curiouser and curiouser as Alice would say. "When you and Tom met at the University, how did you meet? Were you members of any group?"

"We met in a class on the Vietnam War that was taught in the history department." She giggled and said, "Tom had avoided the draft by drinking too much coffee and causing his blood pressure to soar sky high when he went in for his physical. He was pretty proud of himself. Thought he was a radical."

"You two were involved in the anti-war demonstrations, weren't you?"

"Yes, but so was half the campus. The whole French department went on strike. Grève, they called it. I was taking French classes at the time. I thought they were so cool."

"Did you join any group?"

She lifted out a bunch of roses from the vase and started pulling dead petals off the blossoms. "Why do you want to know?"

"I remembered there was a bomb incident over at the

ROTC building. Did you know anything about it?"

She turned back to me and said slowly, "That's so long ago. I have a new life now. I'm not with Tom. I have a wonderful woman lover and I'm going to have a child. I don't want that all dug up. It's behind me now."

I had to be careful here. She was shutting down on me and I needed just a little more information. "I understand and I don't blame you. It was a long time ago. But let me explain why I'm asking." Make it good, I thought, try the truth. "I'm working on this piece about abortion as I told you, but I'm also following up a story on the bombing that happened at the family planning clinic. I was wondering if Tom knew anything about explosives?"

"I really don't want to talk about it." She got angry like she was embarrassed about it. Turning her back on me, she kept speaking. "Ask Tom if you want to know. Ask someone else. I was a kid then. We all were doing crazy things."

"You were picked up by the police, weren't you?" I needed this. If she would answer this question, I could pass the information on to Tennison without any chance of incriminating Gary.

She pivoted on one foot and looked at me, her arms folded over her chest. "Yes, but they couldn't prove anything."

"Listen, I'm sorry to bother you about that stuff. I agree with you. It's a long time ago and I'm sure no one blames you for anything. But if Tom was setting bombs twenty years ago for a cause he believed in then, he might do it again." I wanted to prepare her, because I knew that when I told Tennison, the first thing he would do is dig it all up. Sheila had probably not heard the end of it.

Sheila shook her head, not as if she were saying "no," more like she was trying to get rid of a pesky fly. I knew I was pesky and decided to keep quiet.

Sheila leaned on the counter and her voice got softer and lower. "I feel like I was a different person then. I did things I would never dream of doing now. I was acting out all over the place."

"From what I could see, everyone was."

"I've thought about what Tom is doing now. I mean, I don't think about him a lot, but I've wondered about his involvement with the pro-life movement and I think he just always has liked to be were the action is. It isn't that ideological for him." Sheila smiled and went on, "Before I met him, he resisted the draft because it was the thing to do. I was proud of him for it, but I'll say this, he really got into being confrontational on campus. He joined the army against the war at home. And now he's at the battlefronts of the abortion issue."

"Does he know how to build bombs?"

She stood up straight and put her hands on each side of her back. "Enough of this. Yes, he did. OK, he did. I need to get to work."

"Could I get some flowers?" I asked.

She waved toward the bouquets that were already made up. "What would you like?"

I thought of spring, possibilities opening up, blooming like lilies. Their smell was sweet and heavy and filled with ritual from many Easters. "Do you have any lilies?"

"I have some great pink lilies, Rubrum. Bigger than tiger lilies."

I picked out four on long stems and she wrapped them up for me with ferns. "Thank you for the flowers and congratulations on being pregnant."

"You're welcome." She taped flowered paper around the bouquet and then handed it to me. "Next time you come, just come to buy flowers, OK? I meant it about Tom. Ask him the questions. I don't know him anymore.

I don't even know if I'd recognize him. We have gone different ways and I'm glad." She looked at me carefully and I waited. Right before she turned away she said, "He could be very determined about what he wanted."

20

I KNEW IT was a gorgeous day outside—but I couldn't see a bit of it from my desk. It was going to be in the seventies today and the air had been as sweet as field grass when I came into the building this morning. I didn't want to be at my desk, working on an article about abortion. Today felt inevitable, the kind of day that would roll out in front of me and there wasn't a thing I could do about it but try to stay on board.

The talk with Sandy had really unsettled me and I couldn't decide who I should get in touch with next—Sandy or Tom. She was nuts, but at least overtly; it was harder to tell with him.

And then I was concerned about Paul. I had called him once, but he didn't have an answering machine and I didn't feel like trying all night. But I was anxious to hear what had happened with the police when they had come to search his store. I hoped he had kept his cool and was co-operative with them.

I had started going over my notes on abortion to psyche myself up to write the piece. After reading several books on the issue, I had learned some interesting facts. I pulled them out of the many books I had borrowed from the library and jotted them down. I knew I couldn't use them all but I wanted to put a short history of the abortion issue in the piece:

—In ancient times, the Greeks and the Romans considered abortion as a crime against the husband rather than a homicide. I wondered what it was when the woman wasn't married?

—In 1670 an English judge ruled that if a woman was killed as a result of an abortion, the abortionist was guilty of murder. If she didn't die, the abortion was legal. Interesting way to have quality control.

—In 1812, the first abortion case in the United States was heard and the Supreme Court ruled that abortion was legal with the woman's consent if it was done before quickening, which is when the woman feels the fetus move within her, usually near the mid-point of gestation. This research made me realize they didn't have pregnancy tests and in some instances quickening was when a woman knew for sure she was pregnant. At this time abortion was often called "menstrual regulation."

—Dr. Frederick Taussig, an analyst of abortion patterns, wrote in 1936 that the place of abortion in the U.S. was changing due to "the revolt of womankind against the age-long domination of man," and "to the right of women to control their own bodies."

But the quote that affected me the most, the one I was thinking of using to lead off the article, was by St. Augustine from 1140: "He is not a murderer who brings about abortion before the soul is in the body." That was the crux of all the controversy. When did the soul come into the body? At conception, at quickening, at birth?

For me this was what gave this issue its complexity. Sure, I thought women should have a choice. But in some part of me, and not just the objective journalist part, I did wonder what I would do if I belonged to a religion that believed that life started at conception and therefore abortion was murder. The U.S. Supreme Court, when making the ruling on Roe v. Wade, said they could not make a decision on when life began. And both sides of the abortion issue were, to a certain extent, trying to do what the Supreme Court said it couldn't.

Maybe this is where I should go when I found my anger rising at the men and women of the anti-abortion groups trying to dictate what women could do with their bodies. Go into the complexity of the issue. Reside there for a while until my anger died down. Even the names of the two groups were political statements—pro-life or anti-abortion? Pro-choice or pro-abortion? At the *Times*, it had been decided editorially that we would call each group what they wanted to be called—so it was pro-life and pro-choice.

I work in this fashion, by pulling quotes and writing them all out longhand and stare at them, order them, start to build with them. I was beginning to see a form emerge and started to shuffle around my notes into an order I could use. Many writers manage to do this shuffling on their terminal, but I still like to hold pieces of paper in my hands. I also print out my pieces often as I'm working on them and usually edit on hard copy. But I'm unusual that way.

"How was your meeting yesterday?" B.T.'s voice came from somewhere below and behind me so I guessed he had already settled himself on the stool I kept next to the wall. Sometimes I propped my feet on it when I was working. For some reason, short man that he was, he liked to sit on it. B.T. had no inferiority problem. I twirled around and caught him paging through the latest issue of the *National Enquirer*. He read aloud to me, "Woman gives birth to baby with the head of a dog. Now I'm sorry, that woman should have had an abortion. Don't you think?

Doesn't the amnio test catch such atrocities?"

"No work to do?"

B.T. had his back against the partitioned wall, his feet stretched out in front of him, completely blocking entry to my office. He looked very comfortable. "I'm taking a break from the in-depth, biting, fast-breaking piece I'm doing on the new light fixtures installed on the bridges over the freeway in St. Paul. Actually I was thinking of using this as a basis for a column, kind of a companion piece to the feature you're writing." He held up the picture of a woman holding a baby with the head of a dog crudely pasted over it.

I giggled. "Oh, I'd stick with the light fixtures. I love them. They're elegant."

"Can I quote you?"

"I tried to call you last night."

"I was out."

"Just as I suspected. This new relationship is going to interfere with our friendship."

"Only for a few months and then I'll be through the rosy period and into the blue."

"I needed to talk to you. Sandy Chasen has a direct line to god and he's telling her all sorts of weird stuff."

"Tell me." He threw down the paper and I did. B.T. listened without interrupting, and when I had concluded, he said, "Wow." Then he added, "You gotta go talk to her again. She didn't really answer your questions, just made you think of more. Track her down today and get her to tell you what's going on. Admittedly, it will be in this odd god talk she's got going, but you can decipher it."

"You're right."

* * *

When B.T. left, I tried to work on my article, but my anxiety level had risen from talking to him. I decided to go to

187

the clinic and see if Sandy was there, picketing. After a turn around the office to let Glynda know what I was up to and assuring her that my piece was almost finished, I got in my car and drove over there.

I found a free meter across the street from the clinic. From where I was sitting, I could see some women in front of the main door, walking back and forth, carrying signs and handing out pamphlets. At first I didn't see Sandy, then I located her in the parking lot next to the clinic building.

There were two blonde women getting out of a car and she had walked over to talk to them. Even from this distance away I could tell there was tension between Sandy and the two women. Sandy was gesturing and trying to give them some literature.

After a stream of cars passed, I darted across the street and then stopped on the sidewalk, not wanting to get into the fray. The two women appeared to be sisters and looked like typical Minnesotans—thin blonde hair, frizzed up high into bangs, slightly overweight. One was in her late teens, and she was wearing a University of Minnesota sweatshirt and jeans. She was leaning against the car, staying away from Sandy, letting the other woman handle it.

This woman was a bit older and was pregnant. Medium pregnant, but definitely past the point where it was a question, where you're not sure whether she's simply put on some weight and you'd be embarrassed to ask her. She was wearing sweatpants and a large red blousey top. She was angry and was obviously keeping herself between the younger girl and Sandy.

"Get the hell away," the older woman told Sandy. Turning, she motioned to the younger woman and they both started to walk toward the clinic.

Sandy ran in front of them and then stood right in their path, barring their way to the clinic door. She looked like a salesclerk in a hosiery section of a department store, wearing solid brown walking shoes and again the thick tan nylons that made her look twice as old as she was. I could tell they weren't taking her seriously. Her amulet was outside of her shirt today.

"I will not let you do it," Sandy said.

The older woman walked into Sandy, bumping her with her stomach, and asked, "You and whose army is going to stop us?"

"Your baby. Don't do it to your baby. It's God's gift." Sandy was getting hysterical, her voice rising to a shriek. It was then that I realized Sandy thought the older woman was having an abortion. I found it hard to believe a woman would wait so long.

"Not my god. My god takes care of women," the woman shouted back at her.

"Give it a chance to live."

"Get out of our way."

I was standing on the edge of the parking lot now, not twenty feet from them. I wanted to wait until the women had gone to talk to Sandy. The older woman banged right into Sandy again and this time Sandy grabbed her by the hair.

"Let go of me." The woman was hitting Sandy on the shoulder.

"Rachel, come on," the younger woman said to her sister.

Rachel stood still for a moment, with a disgusted look on her face and said, "This bitch won't let go of me." Then she turned around and slugged Sandy in the face.

Sandy dropped both her arms and started to wail. I moved in, ready to comfort her. She tilted her head up to the sky and said, "God, I'm ready."

She lowered her head and seemed to square her shoulders. I was glad to see she was calming down, but then she

reached into her purse. I couldn't believe what I was seeing. I saw the object in her hand, silver, over half a foot
long, barrel pointed at the two women. I saw it but it took
my mind precious seconds to run through what it could be
and decipher that it was a gun. Sandy had a gun in her
hand and she was pointing it at the backs of the two
women. They didn't know she had it. As I watched, she
ran after them. "Stop, you, stop. Don't go in there."

Rachel turned, ready to make some smart crack, but
when she saw the gun her mouth just stayed open, no
words coming out. I dropped my briefcase and felt frozen,
not knowing what to do. I remembered the words I
learned in life-saving—"reach, throw, row, go." Don't
put your own life in danger if you don't have to. So I decided in the small, rational part of my brain that I wasn't
going to try to play hero and grab the gun away.

Sandy stepped up close to Rachel and yelled, "I know
what I'm doing. I shoot real good. Get back out here."

"What the fuck?" Rachel started to take a step backwards, but Sandy shook the gun at her like a finger and
then shot right over her head. The gunshot sounded like a
giant had taken its huge hand and clapped it alongside the
building. It echoed down the block and Rachel sat down
on the sidewalk and held her full belly. Sandy looked
rather enchanted with the sound she had made and the ef-
fect it had had on Rachel. Holding the gun down at her
side, Sandy didn't look like she was going to shoot again
soon. I started to move slowly around them, trying to stay
out of Sandy's range of focus.

Sandy walked up to Rachel and put the gun to her
brow. "I don't want you to go in there. You can't get rid
of your baby."

"I wasn't going to . . . " Rachel started but Sandy
stopped her. Rachel's face had turned red and sweaty, she
was waving her hands.

"No, I don't want to hear you talking anymore. You swear and take the Lord's name in vain. It's your turn to listen to me. I have a lot to tell you."

The younger girl was standing in the bushes alongside the clinic, crying. She screamed out, "Don't hurt her. Please don't hurt her."

Rachel turned and said, "Sissy, get into the clinic and get some help."

Sandy tapped her on the side of the face with the gun and Rachel turned her head back around. "Don't talk to anyone. You are going to pay attention to me. I have a message from God for you. He has given you a gift that is beyond anything you could dream of, the gift of life."

While Sandy was talking to Rachel, Sissy crawled through the bushes, I guessed she was using them for cover, and made it to the clinic door. Just as she opened it the security guard burst out. I finished walking in a wide circle around Sandy and made it to the clinic door.

"What the hell?" the security guard said. He was staring at what was in front of him like it wasn't real.

I said, "Call 911."

"What?" He turned to me and I could see he wasn't quite taking it in. Even though he had been hired to watch out for trouble, he didn't seem to recognize it when he saw it, or maybe it was just that he didn't know it would take this form.

"She's got a gun. She's already used it once. Don't mess around. Call the police, then come out here and clear the area." He turned and went back into the building. Sissy was sitting on the step of the clinic, crying and biting her fingernails. I crouched down by her. "Listen, calm down and talk to me. I need your help. Was Rachel going to get an abortion today?"

"No!" Sissy turned and wailed in my face. "It's all my fault. I'm the one who doesn't want a baby. I'm only nine-

191

teen. She was helping me."

"OK, that's what I thought. Now, I want you to stay right here. When people come out of the clinic, keep them from walking toward your sister. I'm going to go and try to talk to Sandy."

"Who?"

"The woman with the gun." I turned back to the crisis and saw that Sandy had been busy. Sandy had Rachel kneeling on the sidewalk and praying. As I stepped in closer I could hear that she was making Rachel repeat after her various prayers.

"Dear Father in heaven," Sandy started, then nudged Rachel with the gun.

In a mumble Rachel mimicked, "Dear Father in heaven..."

I waited until the short prayer in which Rachel asked for forgiveness was over. Then I stepped up about three yards away from Sandy and said, "Sandy, I need to talk to you."

Not lifting the gun from Rachel's temple, Sandy looked up at me, "What do you want?"

I could tell she was outside of herself, like in a trance. I needed to pull her back down to earth. Give her some facts. "Sandy, it's Laura, from the newspaper. I had some questions for you and some information."

Sandy looked puzzled. I don't think she was used to getting so much attention. She hitched her purse up on her shoulder and whined, "Can't you see I'm busy?"

"I think you should know that this woman, Rachel, wasn't getting an abortion. She's married and wants to have her baby." I made up the married part. I thought it sounded good and hoped if she wasn't she'd just go along with me.

"Then what was she doing here?" Sandy asked me.

I looked around me. People were gathered by the door

192

of the clinic and there were some men from the car wash on the other side of the parking lot watching us. But no one was moving in. That was good. I needed some time. Again, I ad-libbed, "Her sister needed a check-up. Rachel brought her down. Ask her."

Sandy turned to Rachel who was nodding her head. Rachel rubbed her stomach and said, "I already have a name for my baby. He's going to be called Jason after his grandfather."

"You could name it Jesus..." Sandy started and then sirens interrupted her. The police cars pulled up from both directions and slammed into the sidewalk and blocked the entrance to the parking lot. I had my eyes on Sandy and saw her flinch and retreat into herself again, back into the world of her avenging god. Sandy yanked Rachel up and forced her backwards. Rachel sagged next to Sandy, but by prodding and shoving her Sandy made her walk to her car in the parking lot and they both got inside. I followed a few feet behind. The sirens made it impossible to talk, but I wanted to stay close to them and try to talk Sandy down.

Donna, the director of the clinic, rushed up to me. "What's going on here? Does she really have a gun?"

"Yes, Donna, just keep everyone back. Don't let them go near Sandy and Rachel." I motioned her away and Donna turned quickly to keep people from following me.

As I walked up to the car, I could tell that Sandy was confused. She was sitting in the driver's seat, but she didn't know what to do next. Rachel was sitting in the passenger seat, but they weren't talking. I wasn't sure where the gun was, I couldn't see it, but I had a feeling it was still in Sandy's hand. I had an idea how to get through to her.

"Sandy," I yelled. "Sandy, I know what you should do."

Sandy turned and looked at me, but her face had that

193

serene look that meant she was hearing voices other than simply mine.

"Sandy, I understand why you're doing this. You want to save the babies. Right?"

The word "babies" got through to her. Her eyes focused in on me.

"Well, I think you'd better be concerned. You are endangering Rachel's baby's life."

"Not me," she said, and pointed at herself with the gun. "It's them, those butchers in the clinic."

"OK, I know," I said quietly. I didn't want to get her more riled up. "But right now, I think you'd better think of Rachel's baby. We need to let Rachel out of the car, safely. You have frightened a lot of people and they don't understand what you're doing. You need to let Rachel go. You don't want anyone killed."

"The bomb killed someone. That wasn't what I thought would happen. Things don't always work the way you plan."

Sandy was getting worked up again. I wanted to ask her about the bomb, but this really didn't seem like the right time. I needed to say something calming. "It's going to be all right. You need to let Rachel go and then we can really talk. Everyone will calm down. Let's just calm down." Platitudes, but I had to keep talking.

Sandy didn't say anything. Out of the corner of my eye, I could see a cop easing up into position behind the car and one of the other two cops on the other side of the car. I didn't look at them directly, because I didn't want to draw attention to them. Maybe Sandy was distracted enough not to see them.

"What do you think, Sandy? Can you let Rachel get out of the car?"

Sandy turned and talked to Rachel. I heard her saying, "Will you promise to name your baby Jesus?"

Rachel sat forward in the car and nodded. Her lips were pressed thin and her eyes were enormous, making her look like a caricature of herself.

"That's a good idea, Sandy." I kept talking to her because I wanted to keep her going, not let her slip into a fog again. "Now, I want you to drop the gun outside the car. Switch to your other hand and let it go real easy onto the ground."

"What are the police going to do?" She did know what was going on around her. Good.

"It's fine. Just routine. They're here to see everything goes all right." I paused, then said very smoothly, no jerks in my voice, but a real urging. "Now, put the gun in your other hand." I said it loud so that the police would hear and not freak out when she held up the gun.

Inside the car she lifted up the gun and I couldn't tell what she was going to do with it. It was pointed up at the ceiling of the car, then she held it in both hands. I sighed with relief and watched her transfer it to her other hand.

Suddenly I saw Rachel reaching toward the car door. Sandy didn't notice at first because she was watching me, but then she heard the sound of Rachel opening the door. I watched, then screamed "don't" as Sandy turned toward her with the gun pointing in Rachel's direction.

The gravel slashed behind me and someone ran up and hit the dirt. Then a shot sang out. Sandy's arms flew up in the air. Her whole body leapt up off the seat and her mouth was open as if she were shouting, but no sound came out. Another shot hit her in the chest, clean like a punch and she rolled into it. I was watching it happen and it was like a dance, Sandy's head rolling back, then snapping forward. Her head went down and her body pitched out of the car. I wasn't breathing and then I was gulping in air, mad, so mad. She had been blown away. Rachel moved and whoever was behind me did it. I had been

195

working so hard. I knew Sandy had done it to herself.

I bent down and spit out whatever was evil-tasting in my mouth. I heard two women scream, one after the other and I assumed it was Rachel and Sissy. More sirens were going off behind me and there was the sound of many feet running. I didn't want to look up. I had tried to stop it.

I stayed curled over until I felt a hand on my back.

"Laura," I heard Gary say above me. His two big hands came under my arms and helped me straighten up. "Shit, I'm sorry. What the hell were you trying to do?"

It would be Gary. Of all the cops on the St. Paul police force, he would be the one to take this call and be the one to shoot Sandy Chasen and kill her. I assumed she was dead. I felt like I knew she was dead in my body. Gary had an arm around me and I moved away from him. I looked at his craggy face and wondered if I had ever really known him, what was way inside him, why he was a policeman. "Why did you do that?"

"I'm sorry. We couldn't take the chance. With all these people around, we couldn't let her hit anyone."

I wrapped my arms around my body and looked over to where two men were bent over Sandy's body. "Looks like she's dead, huh? I wanted her to make it. She was crazy, not mean. She needed help."

Gary squatted down next to me. "I'm sorry. It happened fast. There isn't time to think when this stuff goes down. I'm sorry she's dead, but I'm glad she's the only one. And not you." He reached out and patted my shoulder. "Listen, I gotta go sort this out. I'll send someone over to take a look at you."

With those words, I stood up straight. I didn't need anybody to take a look at me. I was fine, not dead, just painfully alive. "No, don't. I'm OK."

Gary nodded and trotted away. There was quite a

scene around the other side of the car. I decided I needed to go take a look. To see the end of it. First I saw Rachel and Sissy hugging each other and crying. Donna was leading them away.

I walked slowly up to the side of the car and the cops were pushing people away, but they didn't touch me. I guessed they knew who I was. I could see Sandy's legs sticking out at an odd angle, a position no one would lay in if they were alive. I walked right up to her and looked down. I was saying goodbye and sorry and wondering where she had gone. Her fine brown hair looked like straw spilled on the tar.

I remembered the game we played when we were kids called "Statue." Whoever was "it" would chase the other kids and when she'd catch one, she got to take them by the hand and spin them. Then she'd let go of their hand and say freeze. However the word caught them, they'd have to stay in that position. Sandy looked like someone had said freeze when she had spun out of the car and she had landed on the ground still twirling.

It wasn't a game and she was dead. I could see some blood, but her body was tilted over, covering the wound. A medical examiner was down next to her, checking her out. Her glasses had fallen off and she looked nicer without them. I watched as the medical examiner began to turn her over. His hands were gentle as if she were still alive and jarring of the wound might hurt her. No one would touch her again like that. The blood was the only spot of color on her outfit. Her amulet was in the blood, all too appropriate I thought.

Suddenly, Bob Scale, the crime beat writer, was standing next to me. He had his notebook out, but wasn't writing anything down. He was staring at the crumpled body of Sandy Chasen.

"Who is she?" he asked.

"Sandy Chasen, Tom Chasen's wife. He's the head of the Lifeliners."

Bob turned to me and tried to keep an even voice. "Holy shit! I suppose you're going to want to write this up."

"No, Bob, I don't want to write this story. It's all yours."

He flipped open the top of his notebook and kept himself from smiling. "Can I ask you a few questions?"

"Sure." I turned my back on Sandy. I had seen enough. I wasn't likely to forget her. "Fire away."

21

THE DAY was still beautiful. Funny how tragedy doesn't change that. The sun lowering itself into a cloud bank looked radiant. The air was so clear and light. It felt as if it had rained, as if something had passed through the air and pulled the stickiness and grime out of it. It was a perfect spring day and it was the day Sandy Chasen had died.

The clinic was in an uproar. Most of the workers had come out of the clinic to watch what was happening, in spite of the police and the director's requests to stay out of the way. Sandy's body was behind the car so it was not easily seen, but the shots had been heard by everyone and the news that a woman had been killed was circulating.

As I walked into the clinic, I heard the reception- ist, who I remembered from my other visits, saying to a co-worker, "You know who she was. That nondescript woman who was here most days, handing out pamphlets. Remember we had to throw her out of the clinic one day? Did you ever look in her eyes? Scary eyes. Pleading or something." I agreed with that description. No one was sitting down in the waiting room. Women were milling about, too stirred up to settle down in the red, blue and yellow sofa chairs to wait. Three were standing in front of the magazine rack, a clump of women were gathered around the desk. I heard Donna reassuring everyone that they would continue with business as usual and apologizing that there might be a longer wait because of the confusion.

Rachel and I talked for a while and she thanked me. I wasn't sure I had really helped the situation. But she assured me I had. "The main thing is you distracted her. You didn't let her spiral out of control. She was really on the edge. When she shot that gun, I just about wet my pants. There were a couple times I thought I was a goner." She rubbed her belly. "Both me and the tyke here."

After some weeping, Sissy had decided to go through with the abortion. Rachel hugged her and told her she was brave. She reminded Sissy that it was why they had come down there and not to let that woman stop her even if she was dead. A woman counselor came out and asked Sissy to come with her.

When Donna Asman walked by, she tapped me on the shoulder and asked if I'd come into her office to talk. I followed her, carefully shortening my steps so I wouldn't run into her. She closed the office door behind me and then slumped behind her desk, rubbing her forehead with both hands.

I noticed the pictures of all her children lined up on her credenza. Two little girls—one Asian with pigtails and one who looked like a pudgy blonde younger version of her mother; they both looked to be around five or six. Then two little boys—one who had very dark black hair and round brown eyes and the other who had curly brown hair and blue eyes. The dark-haired was the oldest and I guessed he was ten, while the curly-haired one was the baby and I put his age at three.

"You looking at my crew? I had those pictures taken at Christmas. Many moments during the day I look over at them and remember why I'm doing this. So that boys and girls can have the right to make good choices in their lives." She turned back and pointed in the direction of the parking lot. "So what happened out there? How did you get involved?"

I gave her an abbreviated version of Sandy's story, just said we had talked and she had appeared disturbed to me.

"I hope this is it. Please god," Donna looked ceiling-ward. "Don't let this stir up any more controversy."

"Amen," I added. This was a prayer I understood.

"That poor woman. What was going on in her mind?"

"I'm not sure, but she wanted to have a child and I think coming here every day and watching woman get rid of their chance to have one was just too much for her."

"I don't agree with that, but I get it." Donna said and then leaned over and took off her high heels. "Pardon me, but these things are killing me. Well, it's clear to me that I'm going to have to demand police protection for the clinic for awhile. This is too much. I can't expect either the staff or the clients to come here and endanger their lives."

"That might be an immediate answer."

"To change the subject, have you found out anything more on the bombing?"

I thought of telling her what Sandy had said before she died, that she was responsible for it. But I decided to give the information to Jarski before I told anyone else. Besides, Asman didn't look like she wanted to absorb much more today, so I told her the little Jarski and Tennison had passed on to me. She looked like she wanted to go home, slide her feet into fuzzy slippers, have her husband serve her dinner, hold her kids and watch something funny on TV.

"I wonder how his family is doing?"

I knew whose family she was talking about. I had been wondering about his older brother all day long. "I think all right. They're a very tight-knit clan, which always helps in times of trouble."

"Oh," she said and sat up straight. "I've been meaning to tell you this. More a curiosity than anything else. Bobby Jameson's name kept bugging me. It was so familiar to me, but I didn't know why. So I checked the files. I found out that Paul Jameson had come close to suing a doctor five years ago when his girlfriend had an abortion here. He was going to try to bring a manslaughter case against the physician performing the abortion. I wasn't the director at the time so I wasn't involved in the case. I don't know what finally prevented him. I assume his lawyer told him he didn't stand a snowball's chance in hell. Anyway, isn't that odd. I suppose it's just a coincidence."

* * *

It was still early afternoon. The incident in the parking lot had taken very little time, considering how it had totally transformed several lives. I was wondering about my own. I needed to go down to the morgue and wait for Tom Chasen. Gary said he had gotten hold of him and that Chasen would be there within the half hour. It was probably worse than rude to question the grieving husband, but I blamed Tom for what happened to Sandy. He had to have known how bad she was, how far out in her mind she was getting. Why had he let her out in the world?

I looked at the parking lot. Sandy Chasen's body was gone. Some forensic people were still milling around Rachel's car. The traffic rushed by on the street between my car and the parking lot. The way it had been before Sandy Chasen had been killed. I felt the urge to go back, to pull time back. But if I backed my car up all the way to the office, I couldn't reverse anything.

* * *

When Tom Chasen walked into the morgue, I almost didn't recognize him. Gone was the aggressive, confident

202

man I had met at his home, who had subdued his wife with a glance. His coat was slung crooked on his shoulders. He had no briefcase and it looked like his arms missed it. His hair was swept over his forehead in a younger style.

He wasn't crying, but he didn't appear to be seeing clearly as he looked around the room without focusing on anything.

I sat on a chair inside the office of the morgue and watched him go past me, then heard him ask at the desk for Gary. I'd already decided to catch him on his way out. I didn't want to get in the way of justice and I knew he'd have more time for me then. I realized how angry I was with him. What had he been thinking to let his wife roam the world in the condition she had been in? When he left the room to go to the morgue, I picked up the paper and turned to see how B.T.'s column had turned out, but I couldn't read. I simply sat still and stared at the pink walls of the morgue's office and wondered about the person who had decided to paint them that color. I hoped if I sat there long enough, I would pull out my notebook and start to work on something.

* * *

Fifteen minutes later Chasen came walking back out with Gary. They shook hands.

"Thanks, I'm glad you told me." Chasen winced. "Will it be in the paper?"

"I imagine. It's news. But ask Ms. Malloy there." Gary pointed at me.

I stood up and walked toward Chasen.

"I guess I owe you some thanks for trying to help my wife." Chasen held out his hand and I looked down at it. Instead of shaking it, I put mine out as if I were pushing him away. While I had been sitting there waiting for him, I went over the notes I had taken at the Conservatory. I was determined to find out what the hell he had done with "the babies."

"You do owe me something," I said, but kept my anger in check. "Actually I was wondering if you'd like to go for a cup of coffee."

He started to angle toward the door. I kept up with him and he explained, "I need to make arrangements, call Sandy's folks. Maybe some other time when all this is over." He threw his hands up in the air to show me how out of his control his life was.

"I understand, Mr. Chasen, but I need to know some things and I need to know them now." We had made it to the street and I stood in front of him, really standing in his way.

"I can't, don't you understand what's happened? My wife has been killed."

"Listen, I truly am very sorry about Sandy. Believe me, I understand better than almost anybody in the world. I was there. I tried to save her. Now, what I need to understand is what the hell was going on with her. She talked to me about you killing babies and either you start talking to me or I'm going to tell the police and write it up in the paper. What'll it be, Mr. Chasen? You have time for a cup of coffee?"

He turned to stone and I didn't care. "Where would you like to go?

"How about Mickey's? It's only a couple blocks away." I pointed up Eagle Hill.

"Fine, I'll meet you there."

"My car's right here. Get in, I'll drive."

Mickey's Diner was an old St. Paul landmark that had been saved from the wrecking ball and now was backed up next to a huge building that made it look like a movie set. It was built to look like an old dining car from a train and it perched on the corner of 7th and St. Peter. I had decided to take Chasen there because it was close, they served good pie and decent coffee, and nobody would notice if I had to scream at him.

It was mid-afternoon and not too busy so we were able to grab a booth next to a window. The waitress came and stood by us. After a quiet moment, she flipped open her orderbook, but still didn't say anything, and certainly didn't introduce herself. Without even looking at the menu, Chasen ordered a diet Coke and I ordered apple pie and coffee. It was as much lunch as I was going to get today. When I had lunch alone here, I liked to sit at the counter and watch the pancakes rise on the griddle. All the cooking at Mickey's Diner was done out in the open.

"What do you want to know?"

"Do you kill babies?" I was going to get him off his feet and keep him there until I found out all I needed to know.

"Are you out of your mind?" He moved forward in the seat, like he was going to stand up.

I reached across and grabbed his wrist. Applying slight pressure, I asked, "No, but was your wife? She's the one who told me you killed her babies."

He sunk down and put his head in his hands. "Sandy was suffering from a syndrome. She was hospitalized for it, but had been doing much better lately. Until the bombing incident. That seemed to trigger her psychosis again."

"Psychosis? What do you mean?"

"That's confidential."

I could tell he was feeling really pressed and I thought I'd change the subject, but not ease up. Just come at him from a different angle. "Did Sandy have anything to do with the bombing?"

"No, absolutely not." He seemed to relax a little with the question. His answer was quick and definite.

"That isn't what she told me." I watched his face. He didn't flinch but his eyes shifted away. I looked away to the church across the street. It was called Assumption Church and was made of old gray blocks of stone. I couldn't believe I was haranguing a widower about his dead wife hours after she had been killed.

"You misunderstood or she was ranting. Sandy was a gentle woman, had never done anything like this before."

"What about the squirrels?"

He took a hasty gulp of pop and looked out the window. He tried to say, "I don't know what you're talking about," but it came out like confetti, shredded words that meant nothing.

"She delivered a skinned squirrel to Christine Larsen, the girl whose boyfriend was killed in the bombing."

"Oh, dear God. I had no idea."

"Mr. Chasen, you had some idea. You knew your wife had gone out and shot a slew of squirrels."

"Yes, but she learned to do that when she was a kid. She'd tan the hides, it was like a hobby with her. I honestly didn't know it was anything more than that. She wasn't letting me know what she was doing. I remember one night she disappeared, but when she got home she wouldn't tell me where she had gone. When it got bad, she saw me as the enemy."

"Why, when she was suffering from delusions, did you let her picket at the Family Planning Clinic?"

"It seemed to make her feel better, like she was doing something. It was an important part of her life. Her therapist said she could."

"Did you let her therapist know how she had been lately?"

"No, not exactly. I kept hoping she'd snap out of it. She was hospitalized for two months last year and when she came out, she was so much better. She had gained some weight. She made me dinner every night. We were happy. I thought everything was better. That we had made it through a hard time, but now it was over."

"So tell me what kind of syndrome or psychosis was Sandy suffering from? What did it have to do with babies?" I thought I'd try again. He seemed like he was talking a little more freely.

"Is this going to go in the paper?"

"No, we don't print things like this in the paper. We cover the news. But I need to know what was going on with Sandy. For myself."

"Well, she had like a postpartum psychosis."

"I thought that happened after a woman gave birth."

"It does. It can also happen, well, they call it a different name really." He looked at me and smiled with great discomfort. "This is very hard."

"I'm sorry, but I need to know it all."

"Sandy was suffering from post-abortion psychosis." He dropped his voice to a whisper.

This thought had fluttered through my mind, but I hadn't ever been able to believe it. "She had an abortion? Your wife?" I was beyond watching my words with this man.

"Yes," he said wearily.

"Why did she have an abortion?"

"Because she had to. We had no choice." He wiped at the sweat on his Coke glass. "See, it all started . . . Sandy got pregnant about three years ago. Only for a few months. Then she had a miscarriage. On the hospital records, they wrote that it was an abortion. That really upset her. I tried to explain to her that it was the medical term for miscarriage, spontaneous abortion. Anyway we tried and she got pregnant again." He stopped for a moment to catch his breath. I was always surprised by how much people would tell me. Once they got past their original ob-

207

jections the story would pour out in more detail than I could use. But I wanted to understand Sandy, so I listened.

"At the end of the second trimester this pregnancy became life-threatening. The doctors explained it to her. I explained it to her. But it wouldn't sink in. She begged me not to let them do it, but we had to. She was my wife, I didn't want her to die, trying to have a baby."

"So she blamed you."

"She was all right after the abortion, but then a few months later, she started dreaming about the baby. She started hearing voices, like God was talking to her. She was a very religious woman and her convictions were strong. She couldn't forgive herself. And she wouldn't forgive me."

I sat there quietly trying to decided if I believed him. It rang true to me, but all I had was his word.

"I could give you the name of our doctor, the one who told us she had to have an abortion." Tom was trying to convince me.

"What is it?"

"Dr. Winslow, she's at St. Mary's."

"I don't think I'll call her, but thank you. I'm sorry for what you've been through. That must have been hard."

"Yes, it has been. And then today. . . ." He stirred in his chair like he was about to leave, but I wasn't quite done asking questions.

"Were you involved in the bombing that happened at the ROTC building in 1970? I talked to your ex-wife about it." I remembered a technique the police used in question. They lied to get the truth. I wasn't lying, but I was hoping Chasen thought I knew more than I did.

He turned ashen. "How did you find out about that?" he asked in a gasp.

"I did some checking. You know the police are going to check this all out too. Do you know something more about the bombing that took place at the clinic?"

He stood up, but the waitress blocked him and handed him the check. There was no space in the small diner for him to move around her. He sat back down. "No," he said, but I knew it meant he wasn't going to tell me anything, not that he didn't know. He pulled out a five and threw it on top of the check.

He sat up straighter and looked at me, "But I'll tell you this. My wife was a martyr for the cause. She believed in what we were doing. The bombing might even have inspired her." He was starting to go into his grand orator pose. I didn't want to see him use his wife's death. It would become part of his mythology. I had felt pity for Sandy in her life and now I continued to in her death.

He stood up to go and this time no one got in his way. I was tired of him. I felt like I had gotten some of the answers I wanted and I had decided to get Tennison to really follow up on him.

As if he had read my mind, he leaned over and stuck his face inches away from mine. "Now, leave me alone. If I see one word of this in the paper, I'll sue you. If you mention this to anyone, I'll come after you. I have a whole league of people at my command. If you're half as bright as I think you are, you know what I'm capable of."

He strutted out of the diner and I didn't turn to watch him go. My pie sat in front of me with only the tip taken off. Eat, I told myself, you need to keep up your strength.

22

I DIDN'T GO back to the office. Even though the work day wasn't quite over, I went home. When I let myself in, it was quiet in the house and the late afternoon sun was slanting in from the back of the apartment. I saw the red light blinking on my answering machine and decided it could glow a little longer. I opened Fabiola's room and lifted her up to my chest. She was warm and sleepy, yawning and lifting her paws up to her mouth. Her pink tongue unrolled, then snapped back inside like a window shade.

I crawled into my bedroom, which was flooded with light. Without even taking off my shoes, I sprawled on top of my messed-up covers and closed my eyes. I wasn't just tired; I was exhausted. I couldn't carry on anymore. I had seen too much and needed to go away.

Hours later the phone rang once and then I heard the distant squeaky recorded voice of someone familiar. The sun had left the sky and the clouds were still holding a faded rose color in their folds. Sitting on the edge of the bed, I shook myself awake. I hadn't dreamed of anything. It was like I had turned myself off for awhile.

Fabiola had tucked herself under the covers, only her tail showing. I reached under and wrassled her and she gave me a pretend bite. When I squeezed her, she bit a little harder. A pinch of reality. I let her loose and began preparations to seriously re-enter the world. First in importance, I needed to talk to Jarski or Tennison and tell one of them what Sandy told me right before she died. But, besides that, the deadline of the abortion story was tomorrow; Bob might want to run some of his story past me; and I wanted to talk to Paul. I couldn't forget what Donna Asman had told me and I couldn't help wonder what Tennison had found at his store.

When I listened to my messages, Chasen's voice boomed out of the small speaker on the machine, giving me the willies. "You need to understand that there's a war going on and babies are dying. Nothing or no one will stand in the way of the righteous. You, Miss Malloy, are the enemy. And there's only one thing to do about that." He hung up. Even though his message scared me, I was glad to have it taped. He must be losing it a little to have said it on my machine, but now I could play it for Tennison.

Next was a message from Paul: "Yeah, Laura, it's Paul. I called. I'm still at work, although we've closed. I'll be here for awhile. Call me. (long pause, with no hang-up) I really need to talk to you." He didn't sound happy and I wondered what had happened during Tennison's last visit.

I grabbed the phone out of its holster, poured a large glass of orange juice, got out notebook and pens and my phonebook. I plunked myself down at my kitchen table, facing the wall, and was ready. This was mission control mode. I would take care of all my calls in one fell swoop. First Jarski. He wasn't in. Next, Tennison. He hadn't called and probably didn't want to hear from me, but I needed to tell someone about Sandy and I wanted to know what I was stepping into when I called Paul.

"Hello, Tennison, Bomb Squad."

"Hi, it's Laura Malloy."

"Yeah, Malloy, what can I do for you?" He sounded

like he knew who he was talking to, but that he didn't care and that he was reading through his mail or some other printed matter.

"You heard about Sandy Chasen?"

"Yeah, that's tough. Heard you were there. That's the breaks. Sounds like she was flipping out. What was her problem?"

"Well, she had been suffering from some kind of psychosis and had been hospitalized last year. Listen, she talked to me about the bomb, right before she died."

"Huh," Tennison didn't seem too interested. I wondered what he was concentrating on.

"She made it sound like she knew about the bomb. That she was in on it somehow. I talked to Tom Chasen for a while today and I'm sure he knows something about the bomb. Have you talked to him yet?"

"No and I don't think we'll need to."

"What?" I asked. "There's more. I think that Chasen might have been involved in a bombing twenty years ago. This looks like his M.O. He makes the bomb and then has a woman carry it to the scene of the crime. The first time he used his ex-wife and this time I think he used his wife, Sandy."

When Tennison didn't respond, a thought occurred to me. "Did you find anything at Paul Jameson's store yesterday?"

He paused and it felt like he was deciding what he would tell me. "Looks like it."

"What?"

"This is off the record, Malloy. We're not ready to break it. You got that?"

"Yes."

"We found a side cutter that could be one that worked on the wiring of the bomb. It's got a nick in the right

212

place. Forensics is still working on it and we should have a full report tomorrow."

"So you think that Bobby Jameson did it."

"Yup, I do. I've kind of thought that all along. It isn't very often that a person picks up a pipe bomb and accidently sets it off. We think Bobby was trying to set it up when you interrupted him, causing it to blow up in his hands."

"What do you mean 'set it up'?"

"He was going to detonate it with a small timing device that was attached to the end of the bomb. It's primitive but effective."

"So he could have been looking up at me when it happened. I remember seeing his eyes and I don't remember him doing anything with his hands."

"Yes, you probably surprised him and threw him off. I think he inadvertently hit the switch when he looked up and smiled at you." Tennison let that sink in.

"Right. Does Paul know?"

"He knows we got something. That's all. We really don't know more than that right now."

"Thanks."

"I see this in print and no police will talk to you again."

"Tennison, give me a break. I've been around. I know."

"Sorry about what happened today. I heard you tried to save her."

"I tried." I hung up and gulped down the sob that rose up in my throat. I felt sad and frustrated. Tennison sure didn't want to check into Chasen, which meant I had more work to do.

I picked up the phone again and looked at Paul's number. It was barely six-thirty. I stood up and did a few leg stretches off the edge of the table. Then I sat down and dialed Paul's home number. After it rang seven times, I hung up.

I called my dad's and even though I knew Christine was there, I was surprised to have a woman answer the phone. "Christine?"

"Hi, Laura?"

"How's it going? Sorry I haven't been in touch."

"It's only been a couple days."

"Oh." So much had happened, it felt like a week. "Yeah, I guess it has. Is everything all right?"

"Yeah, just wait, your dad's got the TV on in the next room. He sure watches a lot of it." I could hear Christine shut the door and then she started talking again. "He and I have been talking and we're thinking of having me stay for a while, and I want to and all, but I would like to get up to the city again and take care of some things and see some friends. I could take a bus. Is that all right?"

"That sounds great. Listen, my dad's the boss. Whatever is all right with the two of you is fine by me. Are you finding enough to do down there?"

"Yeah, well, your dad and I were talking and I was thinking about starting school down here. We get along and I like it all right and they've got a real good program in agriculture. You know, I was raised in the city but I always tried to have a garden. I've been looking at the courses they offer and I think I'd like to try."

"You're going to be a farmer?"

"Not that exactly. There's lots of other fields. Grain specialist. Working on hybrids."

"Sounds good." I realized I felt a little jealous. She and my dad sounded like they got along better than he and I did. She was going to go to school down there and be his housekeeper. I had wanted to get out of Waseca as soon as I could, although when I went back there now I thought it was a nice town. "I'm coming down this weekend. Do you want to catch a lift back up with me?"

"That'd be great."

When my dad got on the phone, I thought I heard more contentment in his voice than I had in quite a while. "How's it going?" I asked.

"Fine. Fine. Was just out raking up some leaves. Christine's talking about putting in some flowers in the old beds out front."

"Sounds nice."

"How are you?"

I was surprised he asked. He usually didn't. "I've been better." I paused. I didn't want to tell my dad about Sandy over the phone. Yes, he'd probably read about it in the paper, but I couldn't talk about it right now. "Dad, sometimes I feel like I'm in over my head."

"Yeah, that happens. But just climb up on a rock or a fence and get a better look."

"OK. I'll try that." I told him I was coming down and then we hung up. As usual, he didn't bother to say goodbye. His phone style was stilted at best. I appreciated his advice. But where to find a rock or a fence?

I looked at the phone and wished I could call him back and ask to speak with Mom. What a blessing when she had been only a phone call away. I often felt the urge to talk over my articles with her, get her perspective. I thought of my dad, watching TV in the living room, a pile of newspapers next to him on the floor, and wondered what my mom would think about how we were managing without her.

I'd often thought of B.T. as a kind of rock-like formation. Maybe he could help me get some perspective. I called him at home. "B.T.?"

"Laura, you all right?"

"I guess so. I collapsed."

215

"I had a feeling. Is there anything I can do?"

"Yes, there is. Could you call Glynda for me and just tell her I'm fine. That I'll be in to work tomorrow."

"Call her at home?"

"Please."

"Yikes, I can't believe how you take advantage of my friendship. I'll call her. So what the hell went on today? Bob said you were a real heroine, but he ended up with the story. Why? Tell me all about it."

"It was Sandy Chasen. She pulled out a gun in front of the clinic and took a pregnant woman hostage. I almost had her talked out of it, B.T., so close. But then they shot her. I guess they had to."

B.T. gasped on the other end of the line. "And you were standing right there?"

I felt that second run through me again, the shots, the helplessness. "I feel like shit."

"Listen, you did more than most anyone else in the world would have done."

"But maybe if I had let the police handle it, they could have gotten her out of there and they'd both be alive."

"Yeah, or maybe they would have freaked Sandy out and she would have shot an innocent woman and then they would have shot her anyway."

"Yeah, maybe . . ."

"What are you doing tonight?" he asked.

"Well, that's what I wanted to talk to you about. Sandy told me she was involved with the bombing right before she died. I called Tennison but he wasn't impressed. He seems to think he's got a hot lead on Bobby. In the meantime, I get this weird call from Chasen, sounded like he was threatening me."

"Don't talk to him anymore."

"B.T., he's giving me the creeps."

"I don't blame you."

216

"When Tom Chasen called me, his voice sounded like it wanted to crush me into little pieces. I feel like something's going to snap. I don't want it to be me. I think Chasen is behind the bombing, but I don't know how to prove it."

23

I TRIED CALLING Paul at his store. The phone was picked up immediately by the machine, which had the pleasant voice of the older woman who worked with him. "You have reached the Tinder Box. We're closed, but our hours are. . . . " I hung up. I had been so sure he would be there.

I wandered into the living room and then didn't know what to do with myself. Standing in the middle of the room, I turned slowly around. The top of my boom-box was so dusty it looked gray instead of black. A poster of a dark, canyon-like New York by Georgia O'Keeffe hung crooked. A few piles of books still were stacked on the floor, the ones that didn't fit into my master plan. The cord from the answering machine was all curled up into a knot. So was my stomach.

I needed to do something—talking to Paul would help. I wanted to know more about that side cutter the police had found and what he knew about it. Why he had tried to sue the doctor. How he was doing.

I went into the kitchen and began to make tea. Empty the old stale water out of the kettle, put it on the stove, light the burner. Unscrew the jar of mint leaves, pick out the stems and crush a leaf between fingers. The sweet woodsy smell of mint hit the air. Put a couple heaping teaspoonfuls in a pot.

When the tea kettle whistled, I jumped. I couldn't stand waiting around. I drank a cup of tea fast and decided to get out of my apartment. I would drive by Paul's home and see if he was there. Who knows, maybe he wasn't answering the phone. I understood that phenomenon.

I changed into a rust-colored sweatshirt and leggings. Pulled on my cowboy boots. Then ran to the mirror in the bathroom. My hair was flat. It was really getting too long. The weight of it pulled it down. I needed about two inches cut off. Bending at the waist, I flopped it over my face and gave it a couple strokes with the brush. Blood rushed to my face and gave it a healthy glow. Two lines of brown under my eyes, enhance their rich glow. Yeah, yeah. Paul said he needed to talk to me. I wanted to talk to him. Chasen was out to get me. Time to move.

When I stepped outside, I looked around, but no one was on the street. I laughed at myself, taking this precaution, but as I had told B.T., Chasen's voice on the phone machine had spooked me. I walked down the sidewalk to my car and felt the cool April air. My boots sounded loud on the cement and I wished I would have worn my tennies. But my boots looked better.

When I turned on to Franklin, there was a lot of traffic, but that was to be expected. It was early evening. I had Paul's address and knew where it was but I had never been there. He lived over on Como Avenue in St. Paul. An apartment, probably a duplex like mine. Not too far from his store. As I turned on Como off of 280 someone came down the ramp behind me. I went five blocks and turned down Paul's street and the car turned also. I couldn't tell what kind of car it was because it was too dark. It could even be Paul coming home, which would explain why I hadn't reached him at the store.

I pulled over suddenly and the car zoomed by me. When I recognized it, I let out a small shriek. It was Tom

Chasen's car—the silver Saab. He was following me. My hands froze on the steering wheel and I choked back a scream. Without waiting to see what he was doing, I spun a louie and headed back to Como. My premonition had been right—he had been following me.

For a second, I thought of jumping out of the car and running into a restaurant. But I kept going. When I turned on Como, I couldn't see any car lights behinds me. I immediately got off Como and took side streets for a ways, zigzagging through old neighborhoods from pre-suburb days—small ramblers, little white cottages. Neighborhoods where kids still used the streets like playgrounds for tag and baseball, reluctantly moving off them as I glided by. After about a mile, my heart slid back down my throat and went to its proper place in my chest. I had lost him.

But I was terrified. I couldn't go back to my place. That's obviously where he had been tracking me from. I found myself on Snelling and turned toward Paul's store. Maybe he was there after all in the back area working on orders, and he hadn't heard the phone. I prayed he would be there.

I drove past the state fairgrounds, saw the space needle that had been built after the Seattle World's Fair, and then pulled into the lot next to his store. A pickup truck sat by the side door. I was sure it was Paul's. It matched his description, an old, dark green Chevy. He had called it a classic. I parked my car next to it, on the side away from the road so no one could see it. Through the glass panel at the top of the warehouse door, I could see a light.

I leaped out of the car and ran to the door. It was locked and there was no buzzer, but I banged my fists on it. No one came. I banged again and then kicked it with my boots. I knew there was a reason I had worn them. Shit, he had to be here, I thought as I danced around in front of the door.

The door swung open, but no one appeared. I stood outside and looked in. A hydraulic lift stood right inside the door, like a giant metal bug with its jaw dragging on the ground. Boxes were piled up to form a corridor.

"Hello," I yelled.

"Laura," came a relieved voice. Paul stepped into view from behind the lift. He must have pushed the door open. "Laura, you came."

I stepped forward and put out a hand to touch his sleeve. My eyes were slowly adjusting to the dark. When I stepped forward, we bumped together and I was bundled into his flannel shirt. It smelled rich with smoke. Then he led me into the workspace.

"Thank god you're here. I'm being followed and I'm scared shitless," I said, the words tumbling over each other in their hurry to get out of my mouth. "This weird guy whose wife just died."

"I'm almost done here. I tried to call you. I wasn't sure. . . ." He trailed off and I looked at him more closely. He hadn't seemed to hear what I had said. His hands were filthy, dirty with something black. He had a smear of it across his cheekbone. His hair was oily and uncombed. He was still a mess. I didn't smell any alcohol so at least he wasn't drinking, but why did I think he could help me? At least this would be a safe place to be until I knew what I was going to do next.

"What's going on here?" I asked.

"I'm working on a project." He led me back to a workbench where an overhead fluorescent light hummed, shedding a pool of light in the cavernous back storage area. "You can sit here." He dusted off a high stool. I sat on it and hooked my cowboy heels over the bottom rung.

I needed him to understand the urgency of what I was trying to tell him. "Paul, someone is following me. A crazy man. His wife was killed today at the abortion clinic and he told me some things and now I think he wants to be sure I don't tell anyone else. What do you think I should do, call the police?"

He lifted his head from his work. "No police," he said.

"Maybe you're right." I tried to see what he was doing. A pile of something that looked like red candy hearts lay on the bench and he was picking them up one by one and dropping them into something else. But they wouldn't be candy hearts, that didn't make any sense.

"Paul, are you getting what I'm telling you?" I heard my voice rise as I tried to get his attention.

He turned to me and smiled. It was lopsided, one side of his mouth going up higher than the other. "Laura, I'm almost done here. I'll only be a minute."

Suddenly he reminded me of Sandy. Like he was in a trance. What was he doing? I stood up and walked over to the bench and saw what he was working on. The candy hearts were actually the broken-off tips of huge fireplace matches. Red bits of sulfur. He had sawed them off and now was dropping them into a short piece of pipe. He was making a pipe bomb. I knew this was one of the ways you could do it.

Tennison's words rung through my ears: "The simplest bombs to make." I felt my brain stop clicking along as one thought flashed on to the screen—maybe he *had* made the other pipe bomb. I had to stop him, whatever he was doing. He had a good grip on the pipe, I certainly wasn't going to be able to wrench it away from him. Instead I wrapped my hands around each other, because I could feel them starting to shake. I needed to get him to talk.

But first I had to stop him from working on the bomb. Questions were flying in my head: Why was he putting this bomb together? What did he intend to do with it? I could feel myself go into interview mode. Start him talking about something neutral.

I looked him in the eye and asked him, "How did it go with the police yesterday?"

"I behaved myself, if that's what you mean." His voice sounded steady. His hands had stopped moving for a moment.

"I was sure you would. It is a jolt, though, to know they can come into your life like that."

"Yeah. I closed the store for the day. Just didn't want to explain to customers why police were swarming all around my place. They brought three unmarked cars and stayed all morning. I sat in my office and listened to them rummage around in the workshop. I thought I'd get some paper work done, but I couldn't."

"So it's over with." I turned back to watch him. He was talking to me, but he kept working.

"Yeah, but." He looked into the pipe. From where I was standing it looked like it was half full. I didn't know how full it had to be. "They took some tools with them. It's making me real nervous."

"Did they say anything?"

"Just had me look the tools over, affirm they were mine, and sign for them."

"Did Bobby use those tools?"

"Don't you start, too. I don't know. Probably. Everybody did."

"Sorry." Don't upset him.

He seemed embarrassed about being short with me and rubbed his knuckles. I stared at him and didn't know who he was or what he had done. He looked like he hadn't shaved in a day or two, his stubble was thick with a bald spot under his chin. The sleeves of his shirt were rolled up and his wrists were broad.

I asked him, "What are you doing there?"

He held the pipe out to me. "This is going to take care

of everything. I should have done it right away."

"It's a bomb, huh?"

"Yeah, I don't have much material left here, but there's enough. Learned how to make these from someone who was in the SDS in the sixties."

"Why, Paul?" I pushed the pipe away. "Why'd you do it?"

He looked up, startled, then his eyes sunk and he shrugged his shoulders. "It's a long story. . . ." He went back to dropping in matchheads.

I waited.

"You want to hear it?"

I nodded.

"Did I ever tell you about Diane?"

"You mentioned her. She was your last girlfriend. She had an abortion, right?"

"You gotta understand, Laura. It's not just my fault. It's Diane's and Christine's. They're to blame."

"What did Diane do?"

"She was fucked up. You know, I loved her, I did. But she had some problems. She liked cocaine. She wouldn't do it all the time, but if it was around she couldn't stop. Otherwise, she was fine. Anyway, she got pregnant and told me. I asked her to marry me and have the baby. It was what my mom would have wanted."

He turned to me and held out his hands like he was holding an infant in them. "We were going to have a baby. She agreed. We had a nice couple weeks. Then she started feeling weird, trapped she told me. She started teasing me, telling me she was going to get rid of the baby." He stopped and his face was drawn, his mouth tight.

When he started talking again, his voice had gone up a notch in volume and he was snapping the long matchsticks in two. "OK, I know it's not a baby, it's a fetus, but in my mind it was a baby. I had even picked out names. One for a boy, one for a girl. I was happy about it. But then one night we fought and she ran out of the house. It was gone by the next time I saw her, she had an abortion." He spit out the last word. "Didn't say anything to me. Didn't ask me what I wanted to do. I was so pissed. Half of that baby was from me. Why didn't I get a say in it?"

"I'm sorry."

I could see that the pipe was close to full now and I started to think about all those match heads together in that small space. What if they rubbed against each other? Couldn't they go off just like that?

Paul went back to work, but now he was cutting a short piece of string. "She had the nerve to come over a little high, confess to me what she did, and ask me to pay for it. You know, I think she got rid of the baby so she could do more cocaine. I honestly do. The abortion split us up. I couldn't get over it. I wouldn't give her any money and then she wouldn't see me anymore. I wanted to get someone. The doctors are all in on this. Why didn't they call me? I was going to fucking sue him, but then, what the hell. It was all over."

By the end of his speech, he was standing up behind the workbench. He seemed like he was on the edge of fear or anger. They're so close sometimes, it was hard to say.

I said, "I get it. I know that when I'm angry, I wish there was someone I could dump it on, to get rid of it."

"Do you know what my baby looked like when it died?" He was searching through his pockets. The pipe bomb was leaning against a vise on the bench. "Let me show you how formed it would have been." He pulled out his wallet and then gently slipped out a well-folded piece of paper. When he unfolded it for me there was a picture of a fetus at ten weeks.

I had seen this image before, looking through all the literature I had gone over for my article, but this particular drawing looked more familiar. I was searching my mind, where? In the office. Then I remembered. It was on the fax. The drawing that had been used to illustrate the fax that had been sent to the newspaper. All that was missing was the gun held to its head.

"That's why it was so hard when Bobby came and told me." He seemed even more keyed up now.

"Yeah." I didn't want to interrupt him. He had stopped working on the bomb and if I could stall him for awhile, buy some time, maybe I could talk him out of using it. Or, at least, get my butt out of here.

"See, he and Christine, they'd been together a few years and they really loved each other. Now, I can understand that Christine wants to go to college and everything, but I told him I'd help them out. She could have had it all, but she didn't want it. Bobby wasn't sure he wanted to have the kid. But I thought it would be good for him, help him settle down. He would have been a good father."

"So what did you do?"

"I did it." He jabbed his finger at his chest.

"Did what?" I asked, I guess, so I could hear him say it.

"I made the bomb."

I looked at him and shook my head. How could Paul be telling me this? I said more to myself than to him, "I thought Tom Chasen did it."

"You know Tom? And his wife Sandy? They helped me when I was going to sue the doctor." He continued, "They had talked to me back then about the possibility of bombing the clinic. And so when Christine was going to get the abortion, I told them. They said this time I should make the bomb. Tom showed me how to do it. He gave me a sheet of instructions." Paul nodded his head to a sheet sitting on the workbench. I glanced over at it and saw that there was a diagram of a pipe bomb with a note at the bottom and a capital T as his signature.

226

"It wasn't supposed to hurt anyone, but it would keep Christine from having the abortion. I told Bobby how to use it. I went over and over it with him. Tom and I planned it so Bobby would set it off right as Christine went in to the doctor. It was going to be a distraction. We weren't going to hurt anybody. It was such a small bomb."

Paul's face grew angry. "He didn't even know how to do that. Bobby fucked it up. He never listened. All I can figure is he had trouble setting it off. He was supposed to go and place it in the hallway before Christine went in to the doctor. So she wouldn't have the abortion. But he waited too long. Then he went and fucking killed himself."

It all tumbled together and made a horrible sense. I took several steps backwards and looked over my shoulder to see where the door was. I needed to get out of here. I knew I should offer Paul some kind of comfort, and try to dissuade him from whatever he planned on doing. But I had to get out. Finally I managed to say, "He didn't have to do it."

Paul turned to me, a wild look on his face, like he had stared in the mirror and seen someone he didn't recognize. "He'd have done anything for me. I was like a father to him. He never imagined anything could go wrong. I wanted to take the bomb there myself, but Tom wouldn't let me. Afraid someone would recognize me. Bobby was sure he could do it. I should never have trusted him."

"Tennison thinks Bobby tripped the switch by accident."

"It should have been me. Me that died, not Bobby. I loved him. But he killed himself and the kid, the baby. He didn't even save his own baby." He picked up the pipe and stuck the string in among the matchheads. Then he opened a bottle of vaseline and smeared a glob of it over the end of the pipe.

"Don't do it, Paul." I stood up and started to back away.

"What else can I do? They know, the police know," he repeated. "Bobby's dead and nothing's going to bring him back. So what does it matter? Right?" He didn't expect me to answer. He was just trying to include me in the conversation he was having with himself.

"Paul, this isn't going to make anything better." I backed up across the room. "I'm leaving."

"Yeah, you better get out of here. This one isn't so little. It isn't huge, but I'll be sitting right here holding it."

I thought of going for the phone. But I knew he could light that bomb faster than I could dial 911 and even if I did get all the numbers punched in and they traced the call, all they'd find would be two charred bodies in a blown up building and that wouldn't help anyone.

"Paul." I was almost to the door. He did look up at me. "Think of your mother. You can't do this to her."

"My mother would be proud. She taught me that abortion was wrong. She'll understand why I did this."

I couldn't argue with him anymore so I turned and ran.

My hands were shaking as I tried to get into my car. I crawled behind the wheel and started the car, then drove out into the middle of the parking lot. Frantically looking around for some help, I saw a phone booth on the other side of the lot. Every inch of me was waiting to hear and feel the explosion as I pulled up to it. I was praying and talking to myself, "Come on, get the fucking quarter, put it in the slot. Dial." The operator picked up on 911. "Send the police to Snelling Mall, the Tinder Box Store." She asked a question or two and then was off the line.

I stood inside the phone booth and started shaking. I had to do something more. There had been no explosion yet. I couldn't stop. I called Tennison's number, just in case he was there. He answered.

"Paul Jameson," I gasped.

"Forensics just confirmed. His tools made the bomb," Tennison told me.

"I know, I know," I yelled. "He just made another one."

I told him where I was and begged him to approach the place quietly. "It's all ready to go, the bomb. All he has to do is light a match. If he hears you coming, he'll do it."

Tennison said yeah, and slammed down the phone without saying goodbye.

I left my car next to the phone booth and started to walk back toward the store. I wasn't sure how big the blast would be if it happened, but I couldn't keep myself away.

The night sky was domed above me. It always was, but I stopped myself from going too close to the store and looked up at it and saw the way it arced above me. I knew that even though it appeared to be curved, it wasn't. It went on forever and we were so small in its belly. But still important, I thought. Whatever it was out there that made us all had to think we were important, too. And it was to this god that I prayed. I prayed that Paul could hold off a minute or two longer, that he had one or two more things to think about before he lit a fuse that would end his time here under the dome of the night sky. I stood in the middle of the parking lot looking up, feeling in that inexplicable way, that if I kept still, I could save him by standing there. So I watched the stars hold equally still in the sky and I heard nothing to disturb the peace, until a car cruised quietly into the lot.

I ran toward it until I realized it wasn't the police. It was the silver Saab. I stood rooted to the ground several yards away, watching as Tom Chasen jumped out of the car. He slammed the door, then stared at me. I was between Chasen and the store and I wasn't sure I wanted to be anywhere near him.

"What the hell are you doing here?" he yelled. "Where's Paul? Is he still in there?" He started to run past me when it dawned on me. Shit, he hadn't been following me, he'd been looking for Paul.

"He's going to blow himself up and it's all your fault," I yelled back at him.

Chasen stopped and turned toward me. I was still between him and the side door. His face was twisted with rage, but I stood my ground. He came right up to me and screamed, "Get the hell out of here. You've been nothing but trouble."

"You made all this happen. If Paul dies, it will be your fault. Your bombs are killing people."

Chasen flinched at my last sentence. Then he stepped toward me and I felt a panic sweep over me. "What do you know?" he asked, grabbing my arm.

I tried to pull away, but his hand had locked on me and as I moved, he twisted my arm behind my back. I felt a tearing in my shoulder and stopped struggling. Metal kissed the side of my neck and I guessed he had a gun. When he started to move forward, I didn't hesitate to walk with him. "So Paul's been talking," he murmured to himself. I felt no need to answer. The pain in my shoulder had moved quickly up my neck and was starting to eat at my mind. I just wanted it to stop.

When we stepped inside the open door, Paul held up the bomb proudly and said, "Tom, I made another one." Paul was holding matches in his other hand.

"Fuck, Paul. Put that down." I could feel the nuzzle of the gun pull away from my neck as Chasen shouted. And, mercifully, the leverage on my arm eased.

"No, I'm going out this time. Nothing here for me." Paul looked down, absorbed as he struck the match and lit the fuse.

Chasen dropped his hold on me and pushed past me

with the gun pointing at Paul. I started to crumple to the floor, but caught myself on one knee. Chasen fired the gun and I heard the roar of it and then a ping as it bounced off of sheet metal behind Paul. Chasen didn't take the time to shoot again but ran out of the building and I scrambled after him. I knew we only had seconds. My last memory of Paul was of him holding the bomb like it was a candle and the flame would tell his future.

A fleet of cars were sailing into the lot. Tennison was already out of the front unmarked police car and had a gun aimed at Chasen, encouraging him to drop his. I kept running until I was near Tennison. Then I turned and screamed, "The bomb."

Chasen was about ten yards in front of the warehouse, when there was a deep, resounding thud and a glare of light from the door. I saw his outline with all the destruction on his back. He was thrown forward to the ground, the building went up behind him and again I felt the insuck of a bomb, the glass shrieking as it was pulled loose, the metal grinding off hinges, the walls cracking and moaning. I covered my ears and crouched on the ground. The first flames of fire shot up from the building and lit up the sky, the stars dimming in the vault above us. Silence followed the cry of the bomb and in that soundless moment I knew that Paul had died.

EPILOGUE

"When the United States Supreme Court made their decision on Webster vs. Reproductive Health Services, they handed the abortion issue back to the states like a bomb set to go off." I read the opening line of my abortion issue feature on a sunny Sunday morning, two weeks after I had watched a bomb blast apart Paul Jameson and his warehouse. The bomb image just wouldn't leave me.

After ten years of writing for various magazines and newspapers, I've gotten over the thrill of seeing my name in print and my ideas splashed across a page, but I still sprawled on the floor and read the whole article.

It looked good, taking up the whole front page of the Variety section. Two photos illustrated the piece and Glynda had let me help pick them out. I wanted them to be just right. One picture was of a pregnant woman, pushing a little girl in a stroller and carrying a sign. The sign reads, "Babies have rights, too." The second picture is of a man and a woman with their arms around each other, walking into a family planning clinic. In neither of the photos are the faces visible, except for the little girl who is squinting at the camera. I wanted the focus to be on the fact that this issue involved real individuals, but they could be anyone—someone we know, ourselves.

The headline ran across the top of the page in 80-point

Helvetica: "Abortion Issue Handed to States—What People Think."

As I was getting ready to fold up the paper, Fabiola ran across it. I grabbed her and explained it to her. "See, I changed a lot of people's names in this piece, Fab, baby, but their ideas are there." Christine's reasons for having an abortion, Tom Chasen's fears of women using it as a means of birth control, Sandy Chasen's religious fervor, Donna Asman's commitment to providing women of all income brackets with a choice, Meg Jameson's Catholic views, and Sheila Langstrom's desire to have a baby, coloring her attitude on abortion, and Paul's question of where do men fit into the decision.

I turned over on my back and let Fabiola go. Staring at the plaster ceiling, I traced a thin crack with my eyes and remembered the day it all started, the walls of the hallway cracking after the bomb blast. Blink, blink, go away. Checking my watch, I saw it was almost time to get ready to go. I was driving Christine back to Waseca to my dad's and then I was going to stay for a couple days. Taking a break.

A grand jury had found that Chasen should stand trial for accessory to manslaughter and a bombing. He'd already been found guilty of illegal possession of a firearm, Tennison told me. Lifeliners had posted bail for Chasen. Lifeliners was, ironically, growing as an organization with all this publicity and I hoped that the trial wouldn't stir up more violence. I had heard that there were police at the Lakeview Clinic around the clock, but I wondered how long the city would provide that service.

The sun played across the ceiling, reflecting off a glass of water on the coffee table. I closed my eyes against the glare of the white ceiling and it was like an old TV set going blank, the white line zipping across the screen and then it's gone.

Selected Mysteries From Seal Press

The Jane Lawless Mysteries

The Twin Cities are turned upside down in these three compelling whodunits featuring restaurateur and sleuth Jane Lawless and her eccentric sidekick Cordelia Thorn.

by Ellen Hart:
HALLOWED MURDER, 0-931188-83-0, $8.95
VITAL LIES, 1-878067-02-8, $9.95
STAGE FRIGHT, 1-878067-21-4, $9.95

The Pam Nilsen Mysteries

Three riveting mysteries, featuring sleuth Pam Nilsen, take us through the world of teen prostitution and runaways, political intrigue and the controversial pornography debates.

by Barbara Wilson:
MURDER IN THE COLLECTIVE, 1-878067-23-0, $9.95
SISTERS OF THE ROAD, 1-878067-24-9, $9.95
THE DOG COLLAR MURDERS, 1-878067-25-7, $9.95

The Meg Lacey Mysteries

From the quiet houses of suburbia to the back alleys and night-clubs of Vancouver, divorced mother and savvy private eye Meg Lacey finds herself entangled in baffling and dangerous murder cases in these two gripping novels.

by Elisabeth Bowers:
LADIES' NIGHT, 0-931188-65-2, $8.95
NO FORWARDING ADDRESS, 1-878067-13-3, $18.95

SEAL PRESS, founded in 1976 to provide a forum for women writers and feminist issues, has many other titles in stock: fiction, self-help books, anthologies and international literature. Any of the books above may be ordered from us at 3131 Western Ave., Suite 410, Seattle WA 98121 (please include 15% of total book order for shipping and handling). Write us for a free catalog or if you would like to be on our mailing list.